"Emily, I've come for

He stood in the doorway a moment watching the petite figure bending over the oven, inspecting its contents. Her golden hair was done, like her mother's, in a bun and parted in the middle. Short wispy tendrils of hair curled appealingly about her heart-shaped face, framing vivid blue eyes, pert nose and determined chin.

"How old are you now, Emily?" His gruff voice held an unaccustomed tinge of tenderness.

She rose and twirled about to face him, wiping her hands automatically on the white flour bag apron that protected her blue muslin dress.

"Why, Mr. Judson! I didn't hear you come in!"

"How old?"

"I was twenty at Christmas." Her blue eyes looked directly into his, not flinching beneath his gaze.

"You'd better let those pies be and get off to your mother to pack."

"What do you mean?"

"She's given her permission for you to marry me."

LIGHT OF MY HEART

Kathleen Karr

Serenade/Saga
BOOKS
of the Zondervan Publishing House
Grand Rapids, Michigan

LIGHT OF MY HEART
Copyright © 1984 by The Zondervan Corporation
1415 Lake Drive, S.E.
Grand Rapids, MI 49506

ISBN 0-310-46592-3

Edited by Anne Severance and Nancye Willis
Designed by Kim Koning

Printed in the United States of America

85 86 87 88 89 / 10 9 8 7 6 5 4 3 2

For Larry and Mary Louise
with love and thanks

And I said to the man. . ."Give me
a light; that I may tread safely into the unknown." And he replied: "Go out into the
darkness and put your hand into the hand of God.
That shall be to you better than light and
safer than a known way."

– M. Louise Haskins

CHAPTER 1

Feb. 4. The night was mild for this month. No winds this morning and I can see the ice begin to break across the bay. Will chance the trip ashore.

Keith Judson pulled hard at the oars. It was not an easy matter to row and guide the unwieldy dory through the narrow channels of water between the ever moving ice floes. Despite the frigid air, he could feel sweat breaking out on his brow. He occasionally freed a hand to wipe it away from his piercing brown eyes, but it clung to the back of his hands and to his curly auburn sideburns and immediately froze.

"Forgive me for being impatient with you, Patience," he sighed half aloud, a habit not unusual for one of his calling, "but, it has been twelve weeks since you took ill on me, and the weather did look to be clearing. . . ."

With incredible strength of will, Judson kept pulling, right on into the tiny harbor town. He glanced at the midmorning sky as he made fast to the pier, then hefted a large, awkward bundle over his shoulder and clambered ashore. He'd better be hurrying if he was to get back the three miles to his island before the weather broke again.

Hastening past the few shops on East Egg's main street, he noticed the warm glow emanating from the big potbellied stove at the back of the general store. Passing horses had churned the usual mud street into knee-deep snowy slush. Determinedly he struggled on, straight to the little white church at the head of the town. The tremulous sound of a wheezing organ made him ignore the small parson's house standing comfortably next to it. Judson stomped up the stairs of the small porch, cursorily cleaning his boots before he leaned on the door and pushed it open. The interior was cold, too—cold as death. Judson eased his burden onto a back pew and bellowed through the tentative Bach fugue.

"Parson! Parson Howe! Put down your music and come. The Lord's work is waiting for ye!"

The organ wheeze stopped and a small, well-wrapped, timid-looking soul appeared. Parson Howe took in the hulking six-footer, dripping amidst the pews.

"Keith Judson! What brings you off the light, and it isn't near spring yet?"

"It's my wife Patience. She's lying here quite froze. Up and died on me twelve weeks past, and I've kept her on ice till the floes broke a bit. She'll be needing a Christian burial. Hard as our life together has been, I couldn't give her to the fishes."

Howe thought a minute. "Knowing somewhat of ye, Judson, I commend your effort. But it will be too cold to put her in the ground here, too. The grave-yard's frozen six foot down. She'll have to wait till the thaw."

"Can ye at least say some words over her? She had a sore-distressed spirit most of her life, and that spirit wants release."

"Aye, that I can do. Come, help me arrange her out back."

An hour later, with Patience attended to for the time being, Judson shook the parson's hand as he kept a weather-eye cocked to the sky.

"You'll not be going off anywhere in the next hour or two, I trust, Parson?"

Howe gave Judson a flinty look. "What? Do you intend to bring me more business before the day is through?"

"I do, indeed." And Judson strode off.

A light sprinkling of snow had begun as Judson walked again down the main street. He automatically quickened his stride into the general store. He had to shake awake the owner dozing by the fire.

"Come on, Ezra, be quick about it."

"Wha. . . ?" Keith Judson! Is it spring already?"

"No. And more's the pity. The snow's coming again and I must get back to the light. Here." He jammed a scribbled piece of paper into Ezra's hand. "I'll be needing these provisions to put on my boat in little more than an hour, and I've unfinished business before that."

Ezra rubbed his eyes and stood up. "Can do, Judson. How's the wife?"

Judson had already turned to leave. "Gone and almost buried." And he was out in the snow again, leaving a bewildered grocer to fill out his order.

This time Judson turned north, to a small house he knew on the edge of the town. In a few minutes he was through the snow-covered picket gate, knocking at the door. There was a pause before it was opened by a middle-aged woman, her graying hair pulled back in a tight bun.

"Keith Judson!"

"The same. Might I have a word with you, please, Mistress Perkins?"

"Well, I suppose so. You might as well come on in. The weather looks bad again. Is Patience looking after your light?"

"No one is looking after the light." He stood uncomfortably in the entranceway, beginning to drip. Not asking him to enter one step further, Mrs. Perkins looked at the small puddle forming near his feet, mentally calculating the damage to her finely polished floor.

"Well, what is it, then?"

"I'll try to be brief. You have five daughters, Mistress Perkins, all near marrying age. I know your husband is off whaling, and bound to continue for another six months or so. I also know he believes in marrying them off from the top. My Patience is dead these twelve weeks and I've just come from saying prayers over her at the church. I must be back at the light by dark and God knows when I'll be able to return ashore again." He paused to let this information register for a moment, then continued. "I'll need your decision now. Will you let me have your eldest to wed?"

"Emily?"

"Aye, Emily. I hear tell she's fierce strong-willed and has turned down some. But I'm willing to try."

Mrs. Perkins looked startled for a mere second, then let her practical nature take over. "If you be needing a wife that bad, you can have her. It will be one less mouth to feed."

"Where is she?"

"She's tending some pies in the kitchen. Go on in— after you remove those boots. . . ." But it was too late. She was talking to his muddy tracks over her beautiful floor.

He stood in the doorway a moment watching her, oblivious to the moisture dripping from his heavy broadcloth overcoat. Her petite figure was bent over the oven, inspecting its contents. Her golden hair was done like her mother's, in a bun, and parted in the middle. But unlike her mother, short curls that had come loose framed Emily's heart-shaped face, vivid blue eyes, pert nose, and determined chin. The strong heat of the room caused Judson to unconsciously unbutton his overcoat, revealing a rather stern, sober black suit in the style of Lincoln, with white linen shirt and a black scarf tie, the overall result rather incongruous with the dress pants stuffed into his almost knee-high work boots.

"How old are you now, Emily?" His normally gruff voice had a touch of tenderness in it.

She rose and twirled around to face him, wiping her hands automatically on the long white flour bag apron that protected her blue muslin dress.

"Why, Mr. Judson! I didn't hear you come in!"

"How old?"

"I was twenty at Christmas." Her blue eyes looked directly into his, not flinching beneath his gaze.

"You'd better let those pies be and get off to your mother to pack."

"What do you mean?"

"She's given her permission for you to marry me."
Then, as an afterthought: "My wife Patience is dead
and I need a woman around the light. Parson Howe is
waiting. We've got to be on the water again within the
hour."

Emily gave his huge, handsome form an appraising
look—from the wet auburn hair and taut, clean-
shaven face with its decisive nose and somewhat
sensitive mouth, down his strong form to the muddy
boots. Then she returned her gaze to his eyes. There
was an appeal in them that contrasted with his bold
manner—a hidden need that touched her deeply.
"It's been decided, then?"

"It has, unless you cannot stomach the look of
me."

He watched as she poured a cup of hot coffee from
the kettle on the stove and handed it to him.

"I've turned down worse and better. But none as
forthright as yourself." She stopped and stared at him
closely for a long minute, brow wrinkled with thought.
Then, apparently decided, added, "Warm yourself
with the coffee while I make arrangements. The pies
should be done with the packing. It will be welcome to
have something fresh for our supper after the cold
boat trip." She paused to watch him lower his frame
into the upright wooden chair, then disappeared.

In her room, Emily silently shoved things into a
carpetbag while her mother fluttered around nervously, finally speaking.

"Daughter, words between us have been scarce
these years. There is much about the lot of woman
you have yet to learn—much that will be hard, even
painful to bear. But now there is no time to speak of

14

such matters. Would that your father were here." She smoothed Emily's bedspread, then reached for a parcel she'd left on the dresser. "Never mind. Here. Take this book. It was your grandfather's Bible, the one he brought with him from England as a young man. The answers to your questions will be there."

Emily accepted it with a smile of thanks, added it to her belongings, then closed the carpetbag. She looked at her mother, unsure of what to say. Her mother fussed with her own apron a moment, pulled a voluminous handkerchief from its pocket, and dabbed at her eyes. "Run along with you. Your man will be waiting."

Emily bent for a hasty, awkward kiss, then left her childhood home, strangely moved, clutching the carpetbag with its worn volume as if it were a lifeline.

It was close to midafternoon when Judson finished loading the provisions and Emily's parcels into the dory, carefully battened them down with canvas and rope to keep out the sea spray, then took Emily's hand to ease her in as well. He impatiently flung a rug in the direction of her knees, picked up the oars, and began to row out of the harbor with a passion. The snow was still falling, even more heavily now, and he knew the sky would darken earlier than usual. If that foolish Mrs. Perkins hadn't decided to turn sentimental at the last minute, running all over town to collect her visiting daughters for the ceremony, they'd be almost home by now.

Home—the lighthouse on Hazard Island, a tiny granite lump thrust up from the ocean off the coast of Northern Maine, eons before. It had been a point of disaster for British, then American shipping, until Congress had finally decreed a light to be built there almost fifty years ago. The Lighthouse Service required an oath to keep his light going every night, in all weathers, and he had taken it. Pray God they'd arrive before the dark, and the onslaught of the winds. He increased the frenzy of his stroking motions.

"Excuse me, please, Mr. Judson . . . husband."

Her words broke through his fierce concentration.

"What is it, woman?" he barked.

She was taken aback a moment by his reaction, then proceeded, "As I am in the bow, I have a better view of the ice. If I turned forward, and if you would hand me that spare oar, perhaps I could clear a path for the boat. To ease your labor somewhat. . . ." She began to falter.

"This is a man's work."

"Perhaps. But cannot a woman make it a little easier?"

There was a noticeable pause as his mind shifted gears with his oars. Then he was helping her to turn, handing her the oar.

"Be careful, woman. I haven't time to fish you up from overboard. The light waits."

"I begin to understand that," she answered serenely. Then she bundled the rug onto the floor, knelt on it with some difficulty because of her constricting skirts, and began the arduous process of shoving ice from their path. It went more smoothly after that. In an hour they'd cleared the shelter of the inner islands and hit the choppy open sea of the outer bay.

Emily pulled in her oar with a sigh, straightened her hunched shoulders, and sat back again upon the bow seat. She was feeling a little apprehensive herself. She'd never been out in a boat in such weather, and certainly not in early February. Especially not with a man she hardly knew. Even the few fishermen who tried to make a living out of the seas near East Egg had enough sense to pull their boats into drydock for the duration of the long Maine winters.

She mulled over the man grunting at his labors behind her, and the life to come at their desolate outpost on Hazard Island. She'd seen the lighthouse once as a child. Her father, during one of his rare appearances home, had taken her on a boat ride over an unusually smooth summer sea. Even in summer it was near impossible to land a small boat on its craggy shores. They'd circled the small island, waving at the keeper and his family, obviously predecessors to her husband. She'd been fascinated with the tall, conical lighthouse, the tallest structure she'd ever seen, and the compact, cozy-looking whitewashed stone house attached to it, both clinging to the moss-covered cliffs of the tiny piece of land . . . *Splash!* Her reverie was suddenly broken by a large wave which washed across the bow in front of her, leaving her very wet and alert.

"Mr. Judson, sir!" She sputtered and shivered, turning about to face him. "Whatever do I call you?"

"You may not call me anything, madam, if we don't sight the island soon!" he shouted back. "Darkness is falling and the wind is rising. Another quarter hour and we are lost!" And he began to pull even harder.

Incredible! thought Emily to herself. *My wedding day and we may both end up at the bottom of the sea. A great pity it would be, too, never having the opportunity to fathom this unusual man.* She was composing herself with the thought that she really ought to remember some prayers when she saw something out of the corner of her eye. *Can it be?*

Yes! The red cross painted upon the side of the white lighthouse had flashed for a moment through the gray and white world of sea and snow.

"Mr. Judson . . . Keith! To the left! Quickly! The island!"

"Which side of it?"

"Eastward! I saw the cross!"

"We might make it yet, but hang on. The currents are fierce."

Now praying in earnest, Emily held on for dear life to both of the gunwales as she felt the boat turn and the currents literally pick them up and try to smash them head on to the rocks some fifty feet ahead. She never saw how they actually made it to the dory-landing place, for her eyes were scrunched shut, waiting for the crash. Instead of the crash, she heard his voice.

"Emily! For God's sake, girl, grab the rope!"

She opened her eyes, saw a rope swinging above her, and reached for it. She caught it and held it with all her strength. In a moment he had shipped oars and snatched it from her hands, clambering for the icy rocks inches from them. In another moment he was upon the rocks, tying the rope to the bow, making fast another, then winching the boat, complete with Emily, at a dizzying angle out of the water. Then his hands were pulling her onto the solid rock. She swayed for a moment in his arms.

"Praise the Lord! We're here!"

"We are that, but not out of trouble yet. Help me to get the dory onto its slip, then we can winch it up from the top of the island, at the boathouse."

The wind was hurling icy particles into their faces, and it was no easy matter to get the boat—which now seemed huge as a whale—onto its wooden track-like slip. That done, they struggled along the almost vertical path to the boathouse platform, where she helped him laboriously pull the boat and its contents out of danger (with the tackle hidden inside the boathouse). Then, Judson pulled Emily fifty yards across the island and shoved both of them through the front door of the keeper's house. There they leaned against the closed door for a moment, relishing the sudden end to the wind's onslaught.

"Is it like this often?" she asked.

"Only six months of the year," he answered, heaving to catch his breath.

"And from what did Patience die?"

He looked startled for a moment. "Pneumonia, I think." Then he gave Emily another look. "And I'll not have the same happen to you. I've no time to show you around now, so you'll have to find the bedroom. Change into some dry clothes, then see if you can get the fires up again before they all burn out. I've got to get that light going."

"But what about your wet clothes?"

"They can wait." And he was off.

Emily was suddenly tempted to just slide onto the floor, curl up, and go to sleep. But she struggled up and out of her cloak and bonnet and searched for the bedroom. She found the kitchen first and took time to stoke the coal fire dying in the stove with the help of an oil lamp she'd found and lit in the kitchen. Then, feeling quite sodden, she climbed the staircase that seemed to have been there all along and walked into the largest room. It took a while to strip off her soggy wedding clothes.

She grimaced to herself. *Some wedding day*. She

removed her best dress—a bold magenta with a frilled, tiered, gathered-behind skirt. It had been a creation of her mother and sisters after much poring through the latest edition of *Godey's Lady's Book* all fall. She remembered with a smile the horrified looks of most of the black-clad widows at the church Christmas social, and their barely disguised whispers to each other about the suitability of such a color and style for one still a maiden lady. *And bound to remain a maiden lady, too,* she remembered thinking to herself then, *for all the suitable available men about.*

Shaking that image out of her mind, Emily next went to work on her undergarments. The corset was almost impossible to get out of without help. This was where her fine new husband was supposed to enter and gently, almost reverently, release her from the tightly bound laces that went down her back, freeing her to gather breath from bosom to stomach. At least that was the suggestion of certain romantic novels she'd managed to secretly procure and read. . . . Finally accomplished with many grunts, she then removed her best lawn shift, decorated lavishly with lace brought by her father from Europe. It had been sewn and waiting in her trousseau chest for over three years now. Lastly, she slipped out of her cotton drawers, trimmed with fine satin ribbons.

Naked and shivering, Emily wrapped a blanket around herself while she added lumps of coal to the bedroom fireplace and ignited it, then hunted for something dry and clean. All the while she was having a little one-sided conversation with God, a habit she'd gotten into as a lonely, eldest child, and found increasingly more comforting as she grew older. She hadn't had any audible answer yet, but she just knew

He was listening. *Well, Lord, here I am. I've really done it this time, haven't I? Any ideas about dry clothes?* There was a large trunk full of what must have been Patience's things, but Emily decided she'd rather freeze to death than don them.

Finally, she found the clean trousers, shirts, and sweaters belonging to her new husband. She gave them a critical inspection. *Well, why not, Lord? I won't exactly look like one of Your lilies of the field, but since You created the weather tonight, I should think neither You nor my husband should find objections to my dress.* They were huge, but warm. She added thick, hand-knitted woolen socks, rolled up the pants legs and felt considerably better. As she walked back to the kitchen, she momentarily reveled in the freedom her body felt in men's clothing. No wonder the opposite sex always appeared stronger and more at ease. No restricting corsets. One could actually breathe comfortably.

Putting aside these surely blasphemous thoughts and touching her waist-length damp hair, Emily began to inspect her new domain, the kitchen. The spacious room's centerpiece was a huge, black cast-iron stove set in the old walk-in fireplace and vented up the chimney. There was also a nice round wooden table and matching chairs made of oak, all of which looked relatively new, but the good points ended there. Green paint was peeling from the walls and cabinets, all was dirty and in disarray, and the dry sink sitting next to the upright water tank in one corner seemed filled with every dish in the house—all soiled. Emily took in the discouraging panorama for a full minute or more. Emily decided that either Patience had been dead for more than twelve weeks, or both she and her husband had been dreadful housekeepers. *Maybe my mother has been right all these years, Lord, about cleanliness being next to godliness. This does seem an unholy mess.*

Sighing aloud, Emily began a quick inventory of foodstuffs. After half an hour she was even more discouraged. She'd managed to start up a large potful of baked beans with the last of the beans, two smoked pig knuckles, and some molasses. But that would take hours to cook. And there was enough coffee at the bottom of the bin to put on a pot. The remaining flour was weevil-infested, and she almost threw it out before deciding she had no choice, at that, and made up a batch of fresh biscuits, keeping her eyes closed during the crucial moments of mixing. She made a mental note to order a flour sifter from the mainland at the first opportunity, and was just removing the biscuits from the oven when her new husband reappeared. She felt his eyes on her for a moment before she turned to see him standing in the kitchen doorway.

"Goodness! You look most dreadful!" she cried— and he did. The red glints in his hair were covered with icy bits. Even his eyebrows looked frozen.

"I've been on the catwalk outside the lantern deck scraping ice from the glass and applying glycerine to the panes to cut down the frost coating." He looked at her again while she digested that unexpectedly technical explanation. "Whilst you . . . you, Emily, look most . . . fetching. I hadn't thought you'd get into my clothes. . . ."

Emily blushed under his intense gaze, then suddenly realized that her hair was still let down, and self-consciously began twisting it into a quick bun before

22

retorting, "They are really most warm and comfortable, and there remains a clean set for you that I've laid out on the bed."

"I thank you for the thought, but the poor cow must be almost dead from pain in want of milking. I'll see to her and try to bring in some of the stores before they freeze in the boathouse." With that, he was gone again.

Fresh milk! thought Emily, pushing the remaining pins into her hair. *Things are looking up somewhat. With a regular supply I ought to be able to make butter, and even some cheese.* In a better frame of mind, she tested one of her biscuits. They had a certain flavor . . . almost nutty.

She sighed to herself again, at the total outlandishness of the whole situation. Well, she *had* given her consent to this peculiar marriage arrangement. That's what came of months indoors in a Maine winter, almost a prisoner with her mother and her precious floors, and her younger sisters' constant prattle about suitors. For a moment it had seemed like escape, and now she'd just have to make the best of it—with the Lord's help.

With that, her native buoyancy returned and she began formulating housecleaning plans for the morrow. Her mental listmaking was interrupted by a distinctive sound she'd been too tired to notice before—a constant clanging, somewhat muffled by the velocity of the winds. Of course! He would have started the fog bells. Visibility must be very poor in what had now turned into a blizzard.

She opened a wooden shutter to look out. It was difficult to see anything but the frost patterns upon the glass, and heavy swirls of white beyond, highlighted by the sweeping light from the tower. With fascination she watched the light, then the periods of darkness. Suddenly realizing there was a pattern to it, she unconsciously began to count . . . Yes! There were three seconds of blinding light, followed by three seconds of darkness, then the light again. Suddenly a bang distracted her, and almost guiltily she closed the shutter on her observation. In a moment her husband had returned with a milk pail in one hand, and her bundle of pies in the other.

She took the pies from him and smiled. "I'd forgotten about these. I'll put them in the oven for our dinner. Would you like a cup of coffee to warm you before you go out again?"

He looked now like a frozen wraith. "No. Once I'm warm I'll not be able to go out again until I rest. I must bring in the supplies first."

"Please—at least a fresh biscuit?"

He looked at her rather oddly for a second. "All right, woman, where is it?"

She handed him one and watched as he crammed it, untasting, into his mouth, before turning about and marching out.

"Uncouth person," she muttered to herself, wishing she had the nerve to use one of her father's saltier expressions. But Christian ladies did not.

There followed a constant banging of the front door as he hauled supplies and dropped them in the hallway. Emily began lugging foodstuffs into the kitchen, then thought better of it. She would clean first tomorrow. No more weevils, if she could help it. So she tended her dinner and awaited the pleasure of his company. And she located a big, wooden bathtub in the otherwise bare pantry down the hall (one

24

couldn't really count three potatoes and five apples, moldering in their bins, and a barrel one-third filled with salt cod), and began to boil water to fill it.

When her husband finally arrived, looking quite finished, she said nothing, just began to help him strip off all of his now almost ruined Sunday clothes, and led him to the steaming bath by the stove. He acquiesced silently, holding on to his dignity and long woolen underwear until her back was turned. Once in the tub, Emily poured water on his almost blue back, scrubbing it to ruddy life. It was her first glimpse at a partially nude male figure, aside from the pictures in a physiology book her father had kept locked away in his desk drawer. She had discovered the key several years earlier and had made occasional surreptitious visits to study its pages.

Pondering this interesting phenomenon before her, she began to hum as she worked, rubbing suds over his chest, carefully avoiding his nether regions.

He opened his eyes once and gave her a sharp look. "You be more knowing than I thought, Emily. Have there been other lessons?"

She blushed deeply and removed her hands. "I only thought to please you. . . ."

He stood up, his back facing her, and shook water around him like a wet dog. "A towel, and my dinner, please. Then I must check the light and wind the bells again. Time enough for acquaintance after that."

Feeling properly rebuffed, Emily served dinner in silence. She broke this silence only twice, first to offer a brief thanksgiving for the meal, and then, after he had worked his way through two cups of coffee and three-quarters of her meat pie, "Excuse me, but is it possible you might have whitewash and a brush? I thought to repaint the kitchen tomorrow. . . ."

"I brought both from Ezra's store today. Patience did not allow my interference in her kitchen, but if you desire, I will help you to prepare the walls. There is little enough to do here during winter days."

"Yes, thank you." And the quiet descended again.

After he'd gone, Emily found her belongings in the hallway. She ignored the damp wooden chest, covered with cowhide and decorated with brass nails, that held most of her trousseau. From the hastily packed carpetbag she pulled out her warmest winter nightgown, a long, full, pink-flowered flannel, with sleeves and tucked front edged in lace. She spread it on a chair near the stove to warm while she cleaned up from the dinner and banked the fire, leaving a bit of heat under her beans to simmer them till the morning. That and the last of the pumpkin pie would have to be their breakfast and lunch till she organized their new provisions. Then she ran up the drafty staircase to the master bedroom. She'd have to see about getting some of this sea-damp out of the rest of the house tomorrow. She fell asleep, still organizing the new housekeeping challenge in her mind. In the press of events she'd almost forgotten to expect a nocturnal visit from her husband.

Emily was awakened by a heavy form flinging itself into bed. As his intentions became obvious, she began to struggle, then fight her way free. She finally shoved his body away and sat upright.

"What, pray tell, are you trying to do?"

"Do? My marriage duty, of course!" He sounded angry, but so was she. "May I remind you that you consented to have me this afternoon? And you didn't seem to find me unattractive.''

"You are really quite handsomely formed," she stammered. "At least those parts of you which I have seen."

"Patience thought otherwise. The only way she'd have me was unexpectedlike. I took all women to be the same."

"Well, I am not Patience. And," she added, "I suspect a little formal notice, a little tenderness, might be pleasant. At least I've read that in some books."

"Books! All Patience read was the Bible." He was propped up now next to her, unsure what would come next. "In fact, the last year or so that was all Patience would do. Sit in the draft with a shawl about her, reading it over and over, especially the more dismal chapters. She had an absolute affinity for Job—before his redemption.''

"I've naught against the Bible. But I feel the Lord is a loving God, not an angry one. 'The love of God is shed abroad in our hearts'—even on this island, in this lighthouse."

"Aye," he considered. "I can see there may be some changes. But I'm too weary to argue more tonight." And he turned his face away from her and quickly fell into a deep sleep.

As for Emily, she lay awake long into the morning hours listening to his breathing, wondering what sort of man she had married and what the future held for them.

CHAPTER 2

Feb. 5. Returned from ashore with new wife in time to tend the light. Fierce snows and gale winds from NNE. Temperature dropped to -5° at dawn.

Emily woke before her husband. She dressed again in the garb of the night before, and tiptoed down the stairs, leaving him to sleep further. She went through the first floor of the house, opening shutters for light, exploring. Besides the kitchen, there was the pantry, a formal parlor heavily draped and furnished with a few pieces of overstuffed furniture, and what appeared to be a very cozy little study. She stoked the kitchen fire and built small coal fires in the other rooms as well. Then she took a moment to look at the small collection of books in the study. They all related to the sea, and seemed to be well thumbed. So! He did read! She would add her precious volumes of the Bible, Shakespeare, and her few books of poetry to these shelves with pleasure.

Slowly, Emily eased herself away from her fascination with his books and took the one doorway she had not entered. It opened onto a small corridor that led to the base of the lighthouse. She pushed open the tower door and began to climb the whitewashed steps, built, like the walls, out of rubblestone. So many of them! And the whitewashed walls, unlike those of the house, had not been smoothed over with plaster. Emily ran her fingers over the bumpy protrusions, not only for support, but to touch their wonderful, variegated textures. The few windows that lined the tower were glazed with ice and allowed only a faint illumination of the steps. The overall effect was like traveling upward through the dim interior of the home of a mountain troll.

She shivered in anticipation, remembering her childhood fairy tales. What wonders would be at the top? Suddenly she reached a small trap door, pushed it open, and entered a new world of brilliance. She had to stop and blink before she realized that, of course, the light would still be working, as it was barely dawn. Then she looked beyond, through the circle of windows around her, and had to gasp for breath. The snow had stopped. All around her was a crystal clear sky; below her, a churning gray-green sea. And the tiny bit of land on which the tower stood poised was an incredible configuration of sparkling ice forms—like the etchings she'd seen of gargoyles from the Notre Dame Cathedral in Paris. It was a veritable fairyland. "Oh!" she gasped, unknowingly aloud. "Oh, my!"

"There's nothing else quite like it in the world, is there, girl?"

Surprised once more by his voice, or perhaps by the awe in it, equal to her own, Emily spun around.

"Keith! You're up!"

"Yes, I overslept. The light should have been out a half-hour ago."

So saying, he edged behind the giant Fresnel lens and began to extinguish it. She watched him, dressed comfortably now in what must be his daily attire—a forest green double-breasted woolen shirt, broad suspenders, and blue woolen trousers that appeared to have seen service on some distant battlefield, and tucked snugly into tall boots now shining with a fresh coat of tallow. He looked rugged and strong. It took an effort to pull her mind back to the business at hand. The light.

"What keeps it burning?"

"Whale oil. The best. It does not harden or freeze in these temperatures like some other oils. You saw the tanks sitting on each level as you climbed up? A lighthouse tender brings fresh supplies of the oil, as well as coal and some foodstuffs when the weather is fair. Maybe three times a year, with luck."

"What happens if you run out?"

"I have enough tanks for a year's supply of the oil. We have never run out of that. I have heard stories of keepers starving from want of provisions, though."

"How could one starve with the sea around? Surely there are fish to catch. And lobsters should be teeming a little way off the island."

"You have a point. But it is near impossible to fish from cliffs such as these, and it is nearly always taking one's life in one's hands to take the dory out through the currents. Yesterday should have taught you that."

"Yesterday was not an ordinary day."

He rubbed the stubble of whiskers on his cheeks. "Yes, I will grant you that." He puttered with the light for another few minutes, then, "Shall I introduce you to the other inhabitants of our island before breakfast?"

"There are others?"

"But of course! Flora the cow. . . ."

"Not named for the savior of Bonnie Prince Charlie after the Battle of Culloden?"

"The same. I see you know somewhat of history," he smiled as he started down the steps.

"A young woman can hardly ignore one of recent history's greatest romances."

He ignored this and continued, "Then, of course, we have the four hens and the rooster. Used to be five hens, but poor Bitsy just froze one night and I was forced to roast her."

"You mean we have regular eggs?"

"Maybe one or two a day—when the hens are in good humor. They should be happy for the sack of corn I brought back for them. By February, the livestock begins to look a little peaked. At least, in the summer, they have a bit of grass to peck at on the rocks."

Feeling some rapport developing at last, Emily smiled happily to herself as she followed her husband down the tower stairs and through the house to don her great cloak and overshoes for the walk around their island. The outbuildings were clustered fairly closely together—a small barn for the livestock, the boat house, a wood and coal shed, a bell tower, and an outhouse. The cow was milked and admired; the chickens, fed. Emily was delighted with the two eggs unearthed from the hay, and promptly collected them for breakfast.

Outside the barn, Keith asked if she'd care to explore the rest of their domain, albeit frigid.

"Yes, please. The kitchen will feel all the warmer on our return. I'd like to see it all."

Looking pleased, he deposited the milk and eggs inside the cottage door, then took her arm and guided her to the western side of the island, from which they could see the long, low outline of the mainland quite clearly in the crisp morning. Emily watched some sea birds swoop across the crests of the choppy waves, looking for their breakfast. Her eyes followed their flight right to the lower ice-covered rocks of their island. Suddenly she tensed and grabbed tightly to her husband's arm.

"What is it, wife?" he asked.

"Look! Below us on the rocks . . . there is something that does not belong there."

He followed her gaze. "It looks to be a body! Wait here. I'll get some rope from the barn."

He was off and back in what seemed only a moment. Then he was tying one end of the rope around the nearest boulder and handing the slack to her. "It is a very steep descent, and I'll need to know something is holding me. I'll also need you to pay out the rope by hand for me." So saying, he tied the other end of the rope around his waist while he waited for Emily to comply with his instructions. Taking a final look, he began a careful descent over the ice-encrusted cliff.

Emily watched with her heart in her mouth as she slowly eased through her hands foot after foot of rope. She'd had to remove her woolen mittens to get a better grasp, and already she could feel the cold biting into her fingers. The husband she hardly knew was risking his life for that of someone lying near the water's edge. It was hard, indeed, to fathom the man. Suddenly she felt the rope go slack, and she leaned a bit further over the cliff's edge. Yes. He had made it! He was leaning over the still form now, inspecting. Suddenly, a shout floated up.

"Emily! There is still life here! But only barely. Hang on hard now! Pull as I climb and wrap the rope around the rock. I'll try to bring him up." So saying, she saw him sling the body on his back for the impossible climb up the cliff. Straining too hard now to think, Emily dug in her feet, praying for strength, and pulled with all her might as slowly, ever so slowly, Keith ascended with his inert burden. Just as she thought she would burst with the effort, Emily saw her husband's blue wool cap bob above the cliff's edge. She gave one last pull, wrapping the excess rope around her body this time, then reached to pull them over the edge. Keith rolled on top of his burden for a moment, then pulled himself together and got up.

"Quickly! Get me out of this rope. My hands are numb." Emily's were not much better, but she finally fumbled the knot open and then they both took an arm and dragged the body back to the house. They unceremoniously left it on the floor by the kitchen stove while they tore off their own wrappings and Emily ran to fill every pot she had with water to boil. That done, she knelt down to help Keith undress the frozen man. Emily began to wipe the ice-glazed head and face with a damp towel, then suddenly rocked back on her heels.

"Oh, no!"

"What is it, Emily?"

"It is Jason Cobb!"

"You are acquainted with this person?"

"Yes!" she gasped, her mind and body reeling.

Keith did not stop to question the level of acquaintance of his wife with this half-frozen stranger, but continued to peel off ice-hardened layers of clothing. Cobb appeared to be in his early thirties, well formed and with a thick growth of black hair and beard. He was close to Keith's height, which was considerable, and he'd certainly weighed enough in the lugging up the cliff. Keith glanced at his wife, who still appeared to be in some kind of shock.

"Emily! If you ever expect to see Mr. Cobb alive again, you'd best run and get some quilts and blankets off the bed."

"*Captain* Cobb."

"What?"

But she was gone up the stairs, giving Keith the opportunity to remove the final layer—Cobb's long winter underwear. He quickly turned him on his stomach and began the life-saving techniques he'd been taught in the service. Then Emily was back, and without further ado they began to bathe and rub the inert figure before wrapping him like a baby in swaddling clothes. A bit of color was beginning to return to the gray skin, and Keith bent over to listen again for a heartbeat.

"He might make it, although he'll be fierce frostbitten."

"What do you suppose happened?"

"I cannot say. Last night's storm was a killer. You say he's a captain? His ship must have gone down entirely. I saw no sign of any remains. We'll have to wait until he talks—if he ever does."

"Will he be all right?"

"I don't know. But we must try to keep him warm. I will bring a mattress from the spare room and put it by the fire in the study. In the meantime, we must go on living. I am still quite cold myself, and could use some breakfast." This last he said rather pointedly.

"Of course. Forgive me. I'll warm some of Flora's milk for the coffee."

Emily tried to tidy up the kitchen after breakfast, but threw up her hands in despair. Keith, guiltily watching her over his fourth cup of coffee, finally grunted and began to move furniture our of the kitchen.

"What are you doing?"

"I am going to paint your kitchen so you will be able to organize it to your liking. Also so you will finally get the provisions unpacked. I have a ham bone in there somewhere that will make a fine soup for our patient. He'll need something clear and warm inside soon if he's to survive."

"Oh. I'd best rub his fingers and toes again." So saying, Emily disappeared once more into the study, leaving Keith to give her vanishing form an appraising look before continuing his own labors.

The rest of the day went quickly, a flurry of activity between the kitchen and the sickroom. Afraid to give the still unconscious man anything to eat or drink for fear of choking him, Emily concentrated on keeping him warm, rubbing life into his extremities. In between, she started a pot of soup and tackled the scrubbing and painting of her kitchen cabinets. By day's end, the kitchen looked brand-new, but would remain sticky and basically unusable for several days. Keith, it would seem, was similarly untouchable. Emily's frequent attempts at making conversation during their shared labors received either monosyllabic grunts, or silence in reply. Finally, Emily stopped trying.

At dusk, just after Keith had gone up the tower to tend his light, Emily went into the study and found her patient semiconscious and feverish. She added more fuel to the fire, wiped his brow, and brought a bowl of broth. Half the bowl had been spoon-fed the captain before his eyes focused on her and he let out his first words: "Dearest Emily!" They were actually more of a sigh before he closed his eyes and went back to sleep.

Shocked by his words, yet grateful for small evidence of returning strength, Emily paused a moment to send up a brief prayer of thanks to God before she picked up the bowl and spoon, arranged the covers, and prepared to return to the kitchen. But Keith was blocking the study doorway, glaring. One look was enough to tell her that Jason Cobb's words had more than registered with him.

With a blush rising unbidden to her cheeks, Emily pushed her way past him, gathering the nerve to throw over her shoulder, "Why such a look, husband? I informed you that Captain Cobb and I had been introduced."

"The word was *acquainted*. Just how well acquainted, pray tell?"

"You chose the word, not I. And what business is it of yours, anyway?"

"I'll tell you what business it is of mine!" He

grabbed her roughly by the shoulders and pulled her close, capturing her lips in a ferocious kiss, the like of which Emily had never known. Unconsciously desiring to respond, Emily dropped the bowl with a crash, soup and all, and began to raise her arms to him, but he pushed her away and stormed off to his light tower.

Emily stood for a moment, shaken, then began to cry softly as she found a bucket to clean up the splatters and shards. Sometime later, her emotions more in control, Emily walked to the base of the tower and listened in the dark to the rising winds howling around it before calling up to him that their dinner was ready.

Returning to the kitchen, she waited for him, but he didn't come. So she ate alone, then went upstairs to rummage through Patience's trunk for some pieces of woolen clothes. These she tore into long strips, getting some satisfaction from the sound of the rending material. Then she gathered up the pieces and settled herself downstairs in Judson's captain's chair by the desk in the study and began to crochet a rag throw rug. Patience might have been cold in her day, but her remnants were going to be put to some use to warm up this house. After a while, with the oil lamp still burning, Emily fell asleep in her chair beside Jason Cobb.

CHAPTER 3

Feb. 6. Yesterday morn found survivor of shipwreck at base of cliffs, one Jason Cobb. Badly frostbitten and mostly unconscious. Fear for his life. Winds blowing again from NNE almost gale force. Temperature -8° at dawn. Rough weather looks to hold.

Emily awoke in the chair, stiff and sore. She felt it must be about dawn from the way the coals had burned down to a dim glow, but she couldn't tell, as the windows were still shuttered. She listened to the continuous howls of wind. Shivering, she gathered herself in the blanket thrown about her, then slowly remembered. She'd fallen asleep in this chair, then. Keith must have spread the blanket, for it was certain from the labored breathing of Captain Cobb next to her that he'd been in no condition to move.

Jason Cobb. Still half asleep, Emily let her mind float back to the summer before, when she'd first met him. She'd heard talk, of course, mainly from her

38

sisters, of the handsome, available captain just home from the sea. Stories about how he'd mysteriously turned up a small fortune and now was the master and owner of his own trim three-masted schooner. Unusual for one his age.

Emily had been out on the moors near town, gathering blueberries and reveling in the lovely afternoon, and in her blessed few hours of freedom from the family chores. Suddenly, topping a small hill, she'd come face to face with a bear cub, also enjoying the berrying. Well aware that Mama Bear could not be far behind, Emily had bolted from the equally startled cub and run back down the hill, only to trip on her skirts and tumble, bucketful of berries and all. She'd been awkwardly trying to salvage the berries and herself when Cobb galloped through the moor on a magnificent roan stallion, spotting her plight and the she bear simultaneously. He'd picked Emily up and slung her behind his saddle and they were off.

The ride had been wild, but no wilder than the moment when he'd stopped on the edge of town to let her down, his hands grazing her breasts before firmly grasping her waist to deposit her on the ground. Then he'd been off on his horse again, grinning his good-by and leaving Emily to shiver with wordless anticipation, a feeling in the pit of her stomach that frustrated her far more than the three berries sitting forlornly in the bottom of her pail. She remembered she'd kicked the pail in an unexplained fury before grudgingly picking it up again and heading home empty-handed.

Her mother had been more than curious about the empty blueberry pail, but had accepted her story of the bears with equanimity.

"Well, Emily, if the Lord chose to put bears on this

39

earth with us, I suppose he meant them to share some of the blueberries with us, too, although I was hoping to have some to put up for winter jam. And there's the church social in two days. The parson always did hanker after my blueberry pie—his wife's can't hold a candle to it,'' she added smugly. Then, almost as an afterthought, but not quite: ''That young curate who does vacations for him will be coming in from Bath.''

She'd paused, then waited for some response from Emily. Receiving none, she continued. ''Seems to me he took quite a shine to you during his last stay . . .'' Still no response. ''You'll not be nineteen forever, Miss Emily Perkins. Just keep that in mind! And you can go back for more berries tomorrow. Whilst the Lord made us both, I'm sure he meant for man to keep the upper hand over the beasts!''

Emily had gone back the next day, more willingly than her mother knew. But though the bears had left her enough berries to fill her pail, there was no return of her dashing horseman.

A racking cough from the bed next to her brought Emily out of her reverie, and she creaked out of the stiff chair to begin the day's duties.

She rubbed down the still feverish and now delirious Cobb, and tended to her own needs, putting on a cheerful yellow gingham day dress for the first time. Then she wrapped a woolen shawl about her shoulders and climbed the steps of the tower in search of her husband.

The light was still on, and he was asleep on a small cot wedged between the light and the windows, arms and legs dangling from beneath a blanket too small for his great form. *So no one had slept in their bed last night*, she mused. And it was more than chilly up here. A glance out the windows told her why. Snow and bits of ice were swirling around the glass in vicious circles, clinging to the panes and making it next to impossible to see the twenty yards out to the sea. Should the light be put out? Perhaps the fog bells should be ringing.

Tentatively Emily approached her husband and gingerly shook him. "Keith?"

He arose with a start. "Whaa . . ."

"The weather is not good. Are the fog bells needed? I think I could remember how to turn them on from what you showed me during our walk yesterday if . . ."

But he was out of the cot, pulling on his boots, pushing her aside. "Thank you, but I hope I am still man enough to look after my light and bells!" So saying, he quickly extinguished the light, and almost ran down the steps.

Emily sighed and began to tidy up the cot. She'd have to find more adequate bedding for the cubicle. And the place could use a good scrubbing down, too. She wondered how often Keith had slept up here while Patience was alive. The blanket and cot covers could use a wash, too. However did one get anything to dry in this weather? Casting one more glance at the inpenetrable blizzard, Emily started down the steep stairs, then stopped with a grin. Of course! The tower well! There was certainly plenty of air circulating here. If she could get Keith to string a long rope for a clothesline. . . . Feeling pleased with her solution of that problem, Emily bounded down the remaining steps to start water boiling for the washtubs, then began to separate yesterday's unused milk for a possible cheese. Maybe she could churn some butter with today's gift from Flora.

By the time Keith, looking like a snowman, returned to the kitchen, Emily was pulling more fresh biscuits out of the oven, and had some of their precious bacon sizzling on the stove next to the coffeepot.

Determined to be cheerful, Emily gave her husband a bright smile and inquired about the animals.

"They are doing as well as can be expected," was his terse reply. "I left the milk in the hallway." And he sat down to fondle a steaming cup of coffee before asking, "And Mr. Cobb?" He still refused to call him Captain Cobb, she noted.

"Our patient is feverish. Perhaps you ought to have a look at him after your breakfast. I am not sure what else needs to be done for him."

Grunting a rather surly assent, Keith proceeded to wolf down the huge breakfast of beans, bacon, and biscuits which Emily had put in front of him.

She chose the moment before he left the table to mention her need for rope, explaining her idea for drying the laundry. "Washday is very much overdue, I am afraid. I'm running out of clean bedding for the patient, and . . ." Instantly she caught her mistake, but it was too late.

"That's all I hear—the patient!"

"But I am only doing my Christian duty. After all, you saved him from the sea and rocks. It would be a pity to have him die now."

"I should have left him there for the birds to eat."

"Keith! You cannot mean that!"

He kept moodily quiet for a few minutes while Emily cleared the table around him.

"All right, woman, you may take that look off your face. No, I did not mean what I said. Any soul saved from the sea is a victory for me in my occupation. I could have only wished it were someone else."

Emily stopped in her tracks to stare at him. Then she began a slow smile. "I cannot believe it! You hardly know me, and yet you are jealous of this poor, sick wretch!"

"It has nothing to do with knowing you. You are an attractive woman, and you belong to me!"

"Sir! I may have married you, but I am no man's possession! I thought Abraham Lincoln, God rest his soul, had freed all slaves!"

"You swore in church just two days ago to honor and obey me!" he thundered.

"I beg to differ with you, sir. I swore to 'love, honor, and obey.' Without the love, I cannot give you an accounting for the rest!" And with that, Emily slammed a few pots for emphasis and stormed out of the kitchen.

She stood for a moment in the hallway, not knowing where to go. She couldn't very well walk out into the storm. Desperate, she grabbed the rug fixings from the study with hardly a glance at the man in the sick bed, and practically ran up the tower steps. At the top she wrapped herself more tightly in her shawl. Only then did she settle down on the cot surrounded by the world of blinding snow-light.

Men! she fumed to herself as she automatically continued the rug in her lap, fingers flying, but eyes unseeing. *Why is it that I cannot live with them, yet cannot seem to do without them, either?* She checked herself a moment to gaze out into the snowy void. *Lord, I certainly would accept a little patience directed this way*. Then her mind sped again to the previous summer, to the second meeting with Jason Cobb . . .

It was a Sunday morning and her mother and sisters had gone off to the church service. Emily had stayed home with a headache. Puttering with the garden in the back yard, she felt immensely better. It was, indeed, a heavenly day. How much more glorious to meditate amongst His growing things than sandwiched between dour faces for four hours. So thinking, she'd been startled by quiet footsteps, and looked up from the flower beds to see Jason Cobb grinning down at her from the fence post against which he was leaning.

He tipped his jaunty cloth cap and straightened the lines of his sporty, checkered tweed Norfolk jacket, looking for all the world like a landed English gentleman. But the piratical gleam in his eyes gave him away. "It is Miss Emily, I believe?"

"Yes, although I don't believe we've been introduced."

"I thought Mother Bear was introduction enough." He grinned again, rather too knowingly. "But I am Jason Cobb. And together we must be the only nonconformists in this godforsaken little town."

"As I've seen none worse, nor better, I hardly think your appellation is precise, Mr. Cobb."

"*Captain* Cobb. And I *have*. I've been to New York, and even London town."

So I can see from your dress, sir, Emily thought to herself, but aloud she asked a bit teasingly, "To see the queen?"

"Unfortunately, not in person, but I did see many fine ladies. None, may I add, who held a candle to your freshness and beauty."

44

"With all that, it took almost a full week for you to find me again?" She couldn't resist asking.

"Ah, forthright, too. I like that in a woman. Will you come with me for a walk, then, since you are so bold with your tongue?"

Emily glanced about her for a moment, a little helplessly. She suspected she was out of her element here, but. . . .

"It should be perfectly safe. The Reverend will drone on for another three hours easily." And he smiled the secret smile of conspirators.

What could she do? He was tempting her, and she succumbed. Soon they were out in the meadows, beyond the prying eyes of the villagers. His arm was crooked about her, ostensibly to support her over the rocks and gullies. When they came to a small gurgling brook, he ceremoniously removed his jacket and placed it on the bank for her to sit upon. In spite of his slightly worldly airs, their talk began to flow naturally, comfortably, Emily speaking of everyday life in her small town; he, regaling her with his adventures. His arm was now around her waist, presumably to support her back, as he sat next to her. His right hand was free, and, with it, he occasionally spun a pebble into the water, causing a waterbug or dragonfly to dash off in alarm. He spoke fondly of flying across the oceans before the mast, of visiting the capitals of Europe to carry on his trade. He was much taken by the wonders of London especially.

"And in London, did you see the Tower where Richard the Third imprisoned the poor little princess? And did you see the royal jewels?"

"Indeed, I did all that, although there's not much left of the Tower now. Used to be an entire castle

45

around it, but that is long since gone. Sailed my schooner right up the river Thames to the great port of London, I did. Rode in St. James Park with the fine ladies in town to await their 'presentations', too.''

"Oh! Do tell me about them! Were they quite elegant?''

"Yes, if a bit standoffish.'' Then, as if that were a mistake, "But I was seen in the proper places. Even had lunch with a lord in his club. Almost got out to his country estate, but the cargo was waiting . . . Perhaps next trip, as we have business together. . . .''

He was looking at her strangely now, with a glint in his eye. And when his left hand mysteriously raised itself and helped to lean her head upon his shoulder, it was not a hardship. From there it was but a small step to find her head nestled in his lap. And he was bending over, his fingers playing with the wisps of curls around her forehead, tracing a light path to her nose, her throat, and from there, the fingers slid down her arms.

In a hot flush, it took Emily more than a moment to catch on to the ultimate direction of his wanderings. Even then, it required a definite effort to put a stop to it, so persistent was he.

She sat upright as gracefully as she was able, and jokingly tried to extricate herself with words. "You are, indeed, a first-class wanderer, sir. Please, I beg you!''

Her protest, she knew, would not go far with this obviously experienced man. But he had a smidgen of decency. Reluctantly he helped her up, dusted off and replaced his jacket, then walked her home in silence. At the garden gate he paused for a moment.

"I would, indeed, enjoy the time to pursue you,

Emily, but I am off on a voyage tomorrow. There is no telling when, if ever, I shall return. Were I a man of the land, I would see to husbanding you properly. See that you choose well. No ordinary man, I think, will be suitable for the job. Your hidden fires burn close to the surface." With that, and another tip of his hat, he was gone.

Her family had returned shortly upon his exit, and Emily had taken to her bed for the rest of the day with her forgotten headache now intensified and combined with formerly unfathomable longings which were becoming all too clear at last.

Emily jabbed herself with the broad tip of her crochet needle and quickly returned to the cold reality of her situation. It was still blowing snow, and she'd run out of rug materials. With a sigh she got up to make another raid on the remnants in Patience's trunk. At this rate she'd have the comfort of a finished rug much sooner than the comfort of the strong male arms she needed. The real question, of course, was whose arms did she most desire?

Keith must have spent the morning working in the barn, for he was nowhere about in the house. Finally, with lunch prepared, Emily bundled up and braved the storm to find him. He was in the barn—in a cozy corner she'd missed before. He'd made a private workshop separated from the stock, and there, in his shirtsleeves, a pipe between his teeth, he was fussing with some kind of pulley apparatus. The little Franklin stove was working at an almost red-hot pitch, and Emily had to remove her cloak almost immediately.

Keith had raised his eyebrows in a silent recognition of her entry, and was now concentrating again.

"What are you doing, sir?"

"Preparing your laundry line, of course. Can't have you falling off the steps while hanging the wash. With this pulley you'll be able to hang and retract all of it from one spot at the base of the tower." He seemed quite pleased with himself, and so was Emily. Impulsively, she gave him a hug, mussing the hair at the back of his neck.

"I've always suspected men would be useful for something," she teased. "I've just never had one around the house long enough to find out."

"I should hope not," he muttered.

"You really haven't a sense of humor at all, have you?" Her sudden good mood was beginning to slip away.

"Never had one around the house long enough to find out," he retorted.

She smiled at his quick answer. "And now, would you care to join me for the lunch I have prepared?"

In silent response, he began to snuff out his pipe.

"The pipe may come, too," she smiled. "I always enjoyed the aroma of my father's pipe on the few occasions he was home."

"Truly? Patience felt it was unfit for a Christian household."

"So you came out here and smoked privately—a little forbidden pleasure."

"Yes." He looked at her a bit wonderingly.

"Well, if it will not destroy that pleasure, both you and the pipe are welcome in the house. It seems harmless enough."

He clamped the now empty pipe firmly between his

teeth. "I'll never understand women." Then he pulled on his overcoat, took her arm, and escorted her through the blizzard to lunch.

As they were stamping snow from their boots in the entranceway, they heard faint groans emanating from the sickroom. They looked at each other, then both raced to Captain Cobb. They found him thrashing about in his blankets, dripping wet and moaning. Then he began to shout aloud.

"The cave, Emmett, steer for the cave! I'm sure I see the opening dead ahead! No! No! The rocks!" And with another groan he fell back onto his pillows, spent.

Emily ran for a cloth and pan of water and began to sponge off the fever sweat. Her movements were thoughtful, tender, as befit a gentle nurse. But her husband apparently interpreted these gestures differently, for his mood changed like quicksilver, and after emitting what sounded like a low growl, he about-faced and stomped into the kitchen. Emily could not help noticing the reaction, but with a softly uttered, "Forbearance, Lord," continued her ministrations.

She was covering her patient with the last clean, dry sheet in the house when suddenly she noticed a difference—a new tenseness—in the sinews of his arms. Looking up to his face, Emily saw that his eyes were open, and there was definite awareness in them.

"Where am I?" he asked, his voice cracking slightly.

"On Hazard Island, in the lightkeeper's house."

"What happened?"

"You were shipwrecked onto our lower rocks and my husband rescued you."

49

"I am not still delirious—I mean, you are Emily Perkins, are you not?"

"Yes, but newly married to Keith Judson, so the name is Mrs. Judson."

"Yes, of course, but"—he looked slightly distressed—"how could that be?"

"Please. Do not concern yourself with details now. You've been quite sick and are still very weak. Please try to relax and I will bring you something to eat."

"But . . ."

"Hush now." She stopped him with the soft touch of a finger on his lips and a smile.

In the kitchen Keith was staring morosely into the cup of coffee to which he'd helped himself. Emily ladled out two bowls of hot soup and placed one in front of him.

"Come, now, they cannot be that bad."

"What?"

"Your moods. I begin to think they are much more dangerous than this rock upon which we sit. Do you really enjoy these black despairs that descend so quickly upon you?"

He looked up at her a moment. "Woman, if I'd been more even-keeled, do you think I'd have chosen to spend my life in this godforsaken manner?"

She stopped halfway to the door with the second bowl of soup, then put it down on a nearby counter for the moment.

"Mr. Judson! I grow a bit weary of your self-abuse. In my brief time here, I have not exactly found you to be the most charming of company, but I have found you to be one of the most resourceful men I have ever met. You have a good mind, are useful with your hands, and exceptionally brave. And there is nothing wrong with a life of service as a lightkeeper." She stopped for a minute to catch her breath, then continued. "Also, this could be a happy place if you'd give yourself and me half a chance." She picked up the bowl again. "I am going now to feed Captain Cobb, who appears to have regained consciousness, in case you are interested. If you want to do something useful this afternoon, you may install that pulley invention of yours, for I'll have to get the washtubs going directly after lunch." So saying, Emily marched off, leaving her husband with his mouth almost, but not quite, agape.

Jason had closed his eyes and dozed off, but opened them again at her approach. She propped him up a bit and spoon-fed the soup, little by little, into his mouth. When the bowl was empty, he gave her a silent look of thanks, rather like that of a cocker spaniel who'd been allowed access to his master's lap. Then the long, luxurious lashes over his dark brown eyes began to flutter, and he was off in a healthy, deep sleep.

Emily sat and watched him for a few minutes, feeling a curious urge to touch once more the thick black curls that wandered so admirably about his well-shaped forehead. The seeming innocence of that mouth was appealing, too. The deep red was returning to his lips. Unconsciously, her mind turned back to her final encounter with these lips. They had not been so innocent then.

It was just before dawn on the morning after their Sunday encounter. She had spent a restless night and, finally, in despair of herself and in spite of her better intentions, Emily had silently gathered her clothes and gone down to her father's study to consult his tidal charts. After the arrival of the fifth daughter, the poor man had given up on a son and had acceded to Emily's thirst for any kind of knowledge. She was an apt pupil and soon was learning the mysteries of the sea. In the years since, she had secretly plotted her father's long voyages in his absence, guessing at where the winds and the currents would take him in his search for whale. Now it was an easy matter for her to gauge the most appropriate moment for Jason's schooner to heave anchor and be off for points unknown. The tide was right just after dawn and Emily quickly dressed and slipped out of the silent house, making her way cautiously, for fear of prying eyes, down to the harbor.

His boat, the *Juliana*, was moored in deep water at the end of the harbor's one long pier. There was some activity in the quickening light between the warehouse adjacent to the pier and the ship. What appeared to be the last of the ship's provisions were being carried down the pier and hoisted onto the ship, to be stowed in the depths of the hold. Emily stood in the deep shadows of the warehouse and watched. *He could easily have been off yesterday,* she thought, *but the Sabbath would not have allowed that.*

Suddenly, she felt her arm being grabbed, and before she knew it, Emily was hauled, not gently, inside the dark pit of the warehouse itself. She spun around silently to find that her captor was none other than Captain Cobb himself.

"Emily! What are you doing here?" he hissed.

"I enjoy a stroll at dawn," she retorted.

"Are you daft, girl?" he whispered harshly. "Have you any idea what could become of your reputation if one of your fine Christian neighbors were to spy you here, seeing off my ship?" He did not wait for an answer, but told her to be completely quiet and still for a moment. Then he shoved her behind a mountain of crates in a far corner of the building and proceeded to finish the supervision of the loading.

Leaning against the crates, her heart in her mouth, Emily finally heard his last order. "That will be all, Emmett and Red. See to the battening down while I take a final look to verify we've missed nothing."

Then he was by her side, his arms tightly enveloping her, his lips seeking and finding hers till she could feel them bruise. Without asking, with neither nonsense nor chivalry, he began to unbutton the front of her shirt dress. Before her lips could open to protest, his mouth was on hers again, murmuring between kisses, "Emily! Emily! Come away with me now!"

Thoroughly shaken and shamed, Emily shoved him away with all her might.

"No, Jason, no! And I'm sorry, too. Truly I am. I didn't mean . . . I should never have come here. Forgive me!"

As she bolted from his touch, clutching her dress, she heard him explode with a stream of oaths and, turning his back on her, he strode to his ship.

Subdued, Emily found a small window with the light beginning to creep in. She clambered onto some boxes to look out, and from there watched the *Juliana* and Captain Cobb slowly sail out of the harbor and out of her life.

Emily had walked home to find her mother stoking the fire in the kitchen stove.

"You are up early, daughter."

"Yes. I felt constricted somehow . . . restless. I took a short walk."

Her mother gave her a sharp look. "Reverend Smythe is going back to Bath tomorrow. I took the opportunity of inviting him for dinner tonight when I saw him after the service yesterday. Didn't bother you with it because of your headache . . ."

"Mother! Tell me you did not!"

"I did, indeed. And if you are as clever a girl as I think, you'll be doing something about it this evening. You won't be nineteen forever, Miss Emily Perkins!"

"No! And I pray God that I won't! It is a most disastrous age!" And Emily crashed a few dishes together rather violently under her mother's gaze, then, relenting, began preparations for the breadmaking.

Soon after, the summer was snuffed out by the onslaught of one of the direst winters in memory, with hardly a respite for autumn. Emily had baked a record number of pies.

"Emily!"

She looked up from her past, the bowl still held tightly in her hands.

"Yes, Keith?"

"Will you not be having any lunch? It grows cold."

"Yes, Keith. Thank you." She got up and trudged back to the kitchen, barely eating a mouthful before starting the water for the afternoon's wash. Every so often she wiped the strong lye soap from her now reddened hands and slipped into the study to inspect the captain, but he slept steadily on, oblivious to the banging sounds echoing from the lighthouse down the corridor.

Just as Emily was about to lug her first basket of wet clothes out of the kitchen, Keith appeared to do it for her. He seemed pleased with the timing, and his invention, and stayed about, cheerfully manipulating the ropes for her.

"With the dampness inside and out, I hope the wash does not grow mold before it dries," commented Emily.

"No fear. I have an old stove lying about in the barn. I thought to bring it in next and stoke it up at the base of the tower to prevent that occurrence."

"But where will you vent the fumes?"

"I think I can cobble together enough pipe to reach the first tower window."

Before she could thank him for the thought, he was out again in the storm.

At least I've given him something to take his mind off Jason Cobb, thought Emily, and returned to her washtubs and wringer.

Dinner that night was very much an affair of leftovers, which Keith ate with apparent relish. Emily then went in and woke Jason to feed him. He seemed stronger, and ate his first solid food. As she was finishing her ministrations, Keith shocked her by coming into the small room and settling himself in the captain's chair by the desk, next to the kerosene lamp. He carefully lit his pipe, then rummaged in the adjacent wall bookshelf, choosing a well-thumbed volume. Emily looked at him expectantly. What would he do next?

He cleared his throat, a little self-consciously at first, then with more aplomb. "As the captain seems awake, and it is Saturday night, I thought it seemly for us to have a little entertainment before bedtime. If neither of you disapproves, I will read a bit from one of my favorite yarns."

Emily could not see the title on the book's binding from her dim vantage point, and her curiosity grew.

"Whatever is it, Keith?"

"A marvelous sea story that was left for me by the captain of the tender *Iris* on his last trip in October. I had not known of the author before, though I now long for his other works. A man by the name of Herman Melville, and this is a whale story called *Moby Dick*."

Jason's eyes lit up, and Emily made herself more comfortable in her chair, pulling her shawl snugly about her. "Do begin, Keith, it sounds wonderful!"

Carefully opening to the first page, he read: " 'Call me Ishmael. Some years ago—never mind how long precisely—having little or no money in my purse, and nothing particular to interest me on shore, I thought I would sail about a little and see the watery part of the world. It is a way I have of driving off the spleen, and regulating the circulation. Whenever I find myself growing grim about the mouth; whenever it is a damp, drizzly November in my soul . . .' " Here he paused to see how his audience was responding.

Jason had painfully propped himself up on one elbow, the better to hear, and now spoke his first words of the evening in an excited whisper.

"It is just so! I never thought it out, but it is just so!" he repeated, then relaxed back on his pillows from the effort.

"You had better continue, Keith, before I begin to talk of wishing to be a man," commented Emily, smilingly.

"You have wished that?"

"And why not? A man may come and go as he pleases, may he not? But whoever heard of a woman setting off to explore the oceans?"

With a look of puzzlement, Keith picked up the book again and continued: " 'whenever I find myself . . . ' " on through the description of a wintry New Bedford and the marvelous meeting with Queequeg. When he looked up again, the lamp was burning low, and Jason Cobb had just given up the struggle to stay awake.

"I think our patient has had enough for tonight, husband," whispered Emily. "I have not, but will have to wait."

Keith looked into her eyes, burning bright with the adventure. *Perhaps*, he thought to himself, *perhaps this is the night to prove to her that being a woman is not all bad*. But then again, he never had been able to prove that to Patience. Ten years wasted. He had not even been able to give her a child. A child would surely have brought a little more joy into their barren lives. His enthusiasm suddenly disappearing into a confusion of regret and helplessness, he swallowed his earlier intentions and said only, "Come, wife," a little gruffly. "The captain is properly tucked in for the night. I think it time for us to do the same."

Then he carefully stoked the fireplace, picked up the lamp with one hand, and, with his other, led Emily upstairs. There he deposited her in the room, helped himself to a candle, leaving her the lamp to undress by, and left for his tower.

Emily, still under the spell of the evening's reading, watched him leave with a small tingle of regret, but said nothing. Instead, she changed into her nightgown and slipped between the cold sheets, then tried to warm herself with the memory of the images so recently cast into her mind by her husband's amazingly strong and stirring reading of the Melville. As she drifted off to sleep, Keith metamorphosed into Ishmael, and she was silently with him, part of his adventure.

CHAPTER 4

Feb. 7. Ferocious snowstorm finally abated at dawn. Temperature at record low of -15°. Winds from NE beginning to calm. Captain Cobb is selectively regaining his right mind.

For some reason Emily slept late. The cold strips of light escaping through the shutter cracks onto the featherbed atop her told her it was well past dawn. Still she was unwilling to jump out and immediately begin the day's chores. And her throat was definitely scratchy. Undoubtedly a legacy of her wedding day's journey. She lay there, contemplating the pillow which should have cradled her husband's head. It was, of course, untouched. But before she could mull over the absence further, there was a knock on the door, and Keith entered, carrying a tray.

"So you are awake," he said.

"Just. But what have you there?" she croaked.

"A small breakfast in bed for the Sabbath. Now if you will just sit up."

"But only invalids have the luxury of a meal in bed!"

"Hush, and follow instructions, please." He looked at her closely then. "I do not care for the sound of your voice. You are not becoming sick on me?"

"Nonsense. Just a little hoarse." She did not wish to worry him, so Emily propped herself up, and was rewarded by a tray plunked on her knees.

"The hens were kind to us this morning."

Before her were two soft-boiled eggs; some slabs of bread, toasted over the coals with lard; and a cup of coffee that had spilled only slightly.

"Keith, how wonderful!" she smiled. "But you must have one of the eggs." She almost added that the other should be saved for the captain, but caught herself in time. It would be sheer foolishness to ruin this peace offering.

He smiled then at her obvious appreciation, pleased with himself. And it only took three more offers of the egg before he sat down opposite her and quickly consumed it, along with most of the toast, then began to talk while she sipped at the coffee.

"It is still quite cold out, but I think the temperature will rise considerably above zero by noontime. You have not had the time to discover it yet, but we have a fine hill going from the cottage to the boathouse, and when the snow is right, and one is quite careful, it makes for excellent sledding."

"Oh, Keith! You have a sled then?"

"Yes, one I made some time ago . . . but never used. You would come, too?"

60

"Oh, yes! If I may wear your trousers again. They *are* so much more convenient than skirts."

"You have my permission," he laughed. "But why not construct a pair more suited to your size, so you do not look so like a lost soul in them?"

"Oho, so that is how I looked . . ."

"Well, in a rather delicious way, I must admit."

"Just you wait, Mr. Judson," she teased, "until I have something made to order. Until then, you shall have to put up with the lost soul." Emily finished the last crumb and pushed away the tray. "You had better let me get about dressing. I've a lot of work to do if we're to take the afternoon for pleasure. The captain might be awake and hungry . . ."

"I've already seen to him, Emily."

"You have?" she asked, a bit startled.

"You needn't act so surprised. I have had some former nursing experience."

"Oh, I am sorry. I was forgetting about . . ."

"Patience. Yes, and maybe just as well. I suppose I could have waited a more decent interval, but after some weeks I had no love for the hermit life, and it occurred to me that by summer you might no longer be available."

With that, Emily was surprised. "But, Keith, you saw me barely twice that I can remember . . ."

"Emily, the companionship, if it ever existed, had long since disappeared from my marriage. You do not begrudge me the distant admiration of a beautiful young girl, I hope?"

"I just . . . I just . . ." she stammered in her confusion, "It just never occurred to me that I might be anything but a quick solution to your problem."

"A solution, yes, but not one made lightly."

"I begin to think you do nothing lightly."

"Perhaps." He got up and removed the tray. "I will leave you now to dress."

And to think. Emily quickly donned her clothes after her husband's disappearance down the stairs. Amazing man! Where had he the opportunity to inspect her at his leisure? She thought hard all the way to the kitchen, and harder still as she took the churn and vigorously prepared butter from Flora's milk, her mind casting back for a memory. Of course! Two times during the previous summer, Keith had brought Patience to the Sabbath services. They had sat in a pew opposite Emily and her family—Patience, prim and dour, obviously taking grim pleasure in the hellfire being preached; Keith next to her, ill at ease in his stiff collar and tight black Sunday suit. The same suit he had worn to marry her.

As she molded her finished butter, then began preparations for bread dough, Emily could not help thinking of the trouble Keith had endured to get his wife to the service. Emily really believed that in his own way Keith had tried to please Patience. Leaving the dough in a huge wooden bowl to rise, Emily was considering what to make for Keith's lunch when she heard groans from the study.

"Good gracious," she said half aloud, "Keith's probably in the barn, and I've entirely forgotten about Jason." She wiped her floury hands on one of the linen towels embossed with, amusingly enough, "U.S.L.H.S." in huge letters. Those towels and the complete set of official crockery, with a lighthouse symbol and the words "United States Light House Service" painted in blue, were among the few niceties she'd found connected with Keith's job. Chuckling over the thought of the ready-made dowry, she trotted in to the captain, expecting to see him uncomfortable, but conscious. Instead, he appeared to be having a relapse of the fever. As she stood before him wondering what to do, he began hallucinating again.

"Yes, Emmett, I agree the weather seems fiercer than usual, but we must get these things off the ship tonight. Tomorrow we must declare to customs. You know the agent seemed suspicious last trip . . ." Then there was some more garbled talk before he began to shout once more, "The rocks! The rocks!"

At that, Emily began to sponge him down and he quieted, then went back to sleep. She looked up to find Keith standing in the doorway.

"Did you hear it all?"

"Yes. I'm afraid I did. I fear our captain's business was not quite straightforward. But if that be so, it should be of no concern to us." But he looked at the captain in repose rather speculatively before saying. "Emily, if you've not yet had the time to notice, your paint is quite dry in the kitchen and pantry. If you'd like some help in clearing the supplies from the hall and stowing them, I stand willing."

Taken aback by the implications of what she'd heard, it took Emily a few seconds to reply. "Yes, of course. Thank you, Keith. But since it is the Sabbath, do you suppose we might have a few moments of prayer together first?"

Her husband looked somewhat uncomfortable at the suggestion, but obliged her by settling down at the kitchen table while Emily went to fetch the Bible her mother had given her. She carefully chose a passage, then looked up at her husband.

"Will you read, or shall I?"

He cleared his throat, then said, "I shall." Then opening the volume to the book of Ephesians, he read: " 'Wives, submit yourselves to your own husbands as unto the Lord. For the husband is the head of the wife, even as Christ is the head of the church . . .' "

Keith raised his head from the words to find Emily's eyes boring into his.

"May I?" she asked.

Keith passed the Bible to her and she quietly paged through it, then began reading in her melodious voice: " 'By night on my bed I sought him whom my soul loveth: I sought him, but I found him not. I will rise now, and . . . seek him whom my soul loveth: I sought him, but I found him not.' "

His request unspoken but eloquently expressed, Emily returned the book to her husband and he continued the reading in his rich tones: "Behold, thou art fair, my love; behold thou art fair: thou hast doves' eyes within thy locks . . . How fair is thy love, my sister, my spouse! How much better is thy love than wine! And the smell of thine ointments than all spices . . ."

He paused and put down the Bible, then lifted his hand to stroke the loose tufts of hair curling along Emily's face. She rose a bit nervously, and closed the Bible.

"I think . . . I think it is past time for the bread to be baking."

He gazed at her without speaking, then returned the Bible to the parlor.

The moment past, the rest of the morning sped by in a pleasant flurry of reorganization while the bread baked. It was noon, and Emily was pulling crusty loaves out of the oven before she realized she'd nothing else prepared for lunch, and said so.

"It is no matter," commented Keith as he seated himself expectantly at the table. "The bread smells delicious, and with the newmade butter, a glass of Flora's milk, and some of your blueberry preserves which we've just unpacked, it will be a feast."

Lovely man, she thought, and sat down to break bread with him. The kitchen looked infinitely better with dishes on the shelves. Perhaps she could brighten up the walls by hanging her small collection of china plates that had been a gift from one of her father's voyages. Thus mentally planning, they ate in companionable silence until they were sated. Then it was time to feed the captain, and Emily warmed a bowl of milk, broke some bread to soak in it, then took it across the hall.

He seemed calmer and was dozing lightly, but he needed nourishment, so she deemed it suitable to wake him. He stared at her all the while she fed him. Then, finished, he asked. "Was there no other body when you found me?"

"No. Should there have been? I mean, were there others with you?"

"Just one. My bosun and companion of many journeys, Emmett Stiles, God rest his soul."

"Your lovely schooner did not go down?" she asked, knowing full well from his feverish exclamations that it had not.

"I hope not. We had it anchored well in the lee of the inner islands. Emmett and I were foolhardy enough to attempt to make for shore in the longboat during the storm."

Well put, thought Emily. *He did not lie and say*

which shore. Aloud, she said only, "My husband and I will check the cliffs this afternoon. The blizzard has finally abated, and perhaps there will be some evidence of. . . ." She did not want to say what she expected to find. The thought of coming upon another body, this time surely dead, did not cheer her.

"Thank you, Emily. And thanks to you and your husband for saving this poor wretch." He lay thinking for a moment, then said, "And the good lightkeeper— is he all you had hoped for?"

Emily hesitated for a moment, unable to answer truly. Blushing at the thought of the celibacy that had been silently imposed on both of them, and again as a vision of the morning's Bible reading rose before her, she quickly answered yes, then busied herself making Jason comfortable before he could see her confusion.

However, Jason's small, sly smile evidenced his understanding before he closed his eyes once more.

Back in the kitchen, Emily was pleasantly surprised to find that Keith had tidied up the few lunch things, and was waiting anxiously to take her outside.

She smiled. "You are like a small child, Keith, eager for his first sled ride."

"I would not know about that, never having had the experience as a child."

"How could that be?"

"Has no one mentioned my sordid past?" he asked, the glimmer of enthusiasm dying from his face. "I was an orphan, probably a bastard child, abandoned by my mother at birth. I was raised in a string of foster homes, treated somewhere between a slave and an indentured servant, depending upon the kindness of the household."

"I'm . . . I'm sorry," Emily muttered, not knowing what else to say. "I was aware of none of this."

"Or you would have turned me down and out as others have done? At least Patience had the grace to accept me with full knowledge of my background, although many's the time she held it over my head later."

Emily walked up to where he was standing, his face averted. "Enough of this nonsense, husband. That was long in the past, and no sin of yours, anyway. I pity more the poor mother who gave you up. It must have been tragically hard for her. And now," she continued in an effort to lighten the proceedings, "and now it is past time to go out and try your sled. This winter light will not last long. Besides, I promised the captain we would walk along the cliffs to seek signs of his missing friend."

He looked up. "Yes, I suppose duty first."

"Not at all. Pleasure first. If poor Emmett is out there, another hour or two will make little difference now."

However, after an inaugural ride down the hill, it was apparent that Keith's heart was no longer in the sledding enterprise, and so they trudged off to check the boundaries of their small world.

At the far end of the island, Emily was surprised when what appeared to be another group of large boulders suddenly shook, showering them with snow and revealing a tiny copse of fir trees.

"Keith!" Emily stood, delightedly taking them in. "I had no idea there were fir trees here!"

"Yes," he broke his silence finally. "Nine of them. Once, the island was completely covered by virgin growth. The first keepers soon demolished all save these to keep their fires going. God knows how these have survived." He surveyed them seriously. "I've tried to nurture seedlings, but the winters almost always destroy them. This past autumn, though, I tried something new. Look." He led her just past the copse to a semisheltered area between the pitiful stand of trees and some rocks. There he brushed several feet of snow away to reveal a white cloth stretched tightly over more than a dozen seedlings, all about six inches tall.

"Wonderful!" she exclaimed.

"More than that. Let me show you." He bent over and pointed out that all but three were fir.

"And the others?"

"Apple!"

Emily looked at the sorry, bare little twigs. "Will they survive?"

"Perhaps. If they do, I will plant them on the lee side of the house, away from the tower. And someday we shall have all the apples we can store for the winter."

Emily looked at the twigs a bit dubiously. She was sure they would never be a threat to the powerful silhouette of the tower. Still, if he could hope enough for this, all was not lost. She straightened with a smile. "We will have apples. And perhaps this spring we could try importing a pear sapling from the mainland as well."

"Why not?" He seemed pleased as he carefully tucked his babies in again. "If we bring in about a ton of dirt and some chicken wire, you might even keep a proper garden."

"Why the wire?"

"To serve as a kind of mesh to hold down the dirt. Otherwise, the winds will scatter it in short order."

"And I thought it was hard to scratch out a garden in the rocky soil at home."

"Never forget that this island was made for the gulls, not for man." He stood up and took her mittened hand. "We'd best get moving now before we get too cold. We still have a few rocks to look at."

And so they continued around the circumference of their domain, ending just above the boathouse.

"We'll have to climb down here. Quite often, debris catches in the small inlet where the boat is launched." He looked at her. "Unless, of course, you prefer returning to the house to warm up."

"No. I want to go with you. I have not seen it since the night we arrived, and then it was too dark and stormy to see anything." They started down then, along the slip tracks, Emily thinking about their first night. Could it have been only three days ago? It seemed at least a year. In these three days her mind and heart had been rocked back and forth more than in all of her twenty years. Was this a necessary part of being married, or was it just growing up? She tripped, mulling over the question, and after brushing the snow off her knees, continued down the steep path with more respect for the terrain. A few yards before the path ended in the sea, Keith had let go of her hand. When she caught up, he was kneeling on the farthest rocks, grasping for something.

"What is it? What have you found?"

He was hauling up a rectangular wooden crate, its dimensions about two by three feet, and she rushed to help him.

"I don't know. I guess we'll have to open it and

see. Might as well do it here. If the contents are waterlogged beyond use, we'll just toss the whole thing back into the sea." He began to pry at the boards with the long blade of his knife which he usually carried in a sheath hanging from his suspender clip.

"Found a crate of Spanish oranges once," he said hopefully. "They were delicious. And we never had a healthier winter. That was about five years back, though," he added, dislodging the first board with a crack. He handed it to Emily. "Here, hang onto the pieces. It's not bad wood. Might be able to build something out of it someday."

Keith continued to pry at the crate carefully, while Emily danced about from a combination of the cold and impatience. Finally, he pulled off the remaining top board, and, before removing the sea-matted straw which covered the contents, stopped and began refilling his pipe.

"For heaven's sake, what are you doing?"

"Filling my pipe," he answered placidly.

"I can see that! But however can you stand the suspense? It is killing me."

"So I see, my dear. But there is little enough drama around here—at least until recently—and I was merely prolonging the pleasure. Think, now. For a moment or two, we can imagine all the treasures of the world to reside in this modest crate. But once the straw is removed, the surprise will be gone. Is it not better to steal a moment of anticipatory pleasure?" And he leisurely ignited and drew on the pipe, having a bit of trouble keeping the wooden match shielded from the winds.

"All right, be a romantic if you must. I'll just sit on

this rock and turn into a lump of ice." And she sat on the nearest spume-frozen outcropping, then began to cough.

He looked at her with some concern. "Forgive me. I had, for a moment, forgotten the cold. All right. Shall you remove the straw, or shall I?"

Emily could hardly restrain herself, but said, "You, please."

So Keith tightly clamped the pipe between his teeth, and bent over for the operation. It only took a second to reveal a row of tightly corked and wax-sealed bottles lying neatly and uninjured in their bed of straw. After a bit of rooting, Keith discovered a total of three layers of bottles, thirty-six in all. He pulled one out to inspect. A soggy layer of flimsy paper which had been attached fell off in his hand. He held it up to the now diminishing light, then called to Emily, who was already standing behind his shoulder.

"Can you decipher this?"

"A . . . P . . . O . . . R . . . T . . . O. *Aporto*."

"That's what I make of it, too." He carefully put the bottle and label back into the crate. "It would appear that we've been delivered a fair supply of Portugese port, compliments of the sea." He chuckled.

"What is so funny?"

"Patience, may she rest in peace, will probably be turning in her grave if she has one yet. There's not been a drop of alcohol on this island in almost ten years."

"I . . . a-choo! . . . I've had no experience with it myself. My father used to keep a bottle in his study during visits home, for medicinal purposes, he said. Mother never allowed the girls near, though. She was

71

dead set against any form of alcohol. She was, in fact, for some time the vice president of the local Temperance League." Emily continued to ruminate with another sneeze as Keith repacked the case.

"Well, Emily, this night you shall have a taste. I do not like the sound of your sneezes. A glass would not hurt the captain, either. I hear tell it is very therapeutic for colds and fevers." And chuckling some more, he hoisted the crate on his shoulder for the trek up to the cottage. "Come along, Emily, I'm anxious to learn if there's been a sea-change in the stuff since last I met it."

Emily slipped and slid behind Keith, pleased at how the "treasure" had cheered him. From conversations overheard between her mother's friends she'd caught wind of how alcohol could affect a man. Something about its aphrodisiac qualities if imbibed to some excess. Shivering with the cold and a mild concern at the potential prospects, Emily was soon entering the cottage behind Keith.

In short order their outerwear was removed and Emily was warming herself by the kitchen stove while Keith surveyed his booty, chose a bottle, broke its seal, then poured a bit of the reddish-brownish liquid into a cup.

"Drink up, Emily," he said, handing her the cup.

"Now, before dinner?"

"And why not? It's medicine you'll be needing to ward off that cold you're developing. I'll not have a second invalid on my hands."

"I just thought. . . ."

"I'm not trying to ruin your upbringing, girl. If you've moral qualms, I know for a fact that most

72

patent cough medicines are at least 70 percent alcohol.''

Visions of her mother's temperance banner swam before her. Then she sneezed again, followed by a rattling cough. ''All right, just a sip, then.''

At first she just smelled. Surprised by the sweetness of the aroma, she tasted. It flowed through her mouth and down her throat smoothly, like molten gold. Then she waited, expectant. Yes, there was a bit of a tingle all the way to her stomach, but quite a pleasant one.

''Umm. Tastes better than 'Hall's Coco Wine' which mother keeps for sore throats and influenza.'' Emily tasted again.

They were both sitting at the table now. ''We will store the bottles in the pantry on their sides. I think the cork will last longer that way. We can reserve the bottles for medicinal use.''

Emily began to feel a lovely all-over glow. ''I do feel nice. And my throat is not so scratchy. Do you suppose it was the afternoon in the open air?''

''Quite possibly.'' His usually tanned complexion was taking on a bit of a ruddy aspect as well. He moved his chair next to hers. ''You know, you really have lovely hair. I have been longing to see it loose again. The small glimpse on our wedding night was not enough.'' His free hand slipped up to her neck, giving it a fleeting caress as he gently, though a bit clumsily, began to pull out her hairpins.

Emily felt the glow more strongly. She patted her hair, coincidentally pulling out a pin he'd missed. ''I am glad it pleases you.''

Suddenly blond tresses were cascading over his hand. His other hand, disengaging itself from its cup, was raised to her face as well, touching nose, eyelids,

73

cheeks, following the strands of hair down to her shoulders. Before she knew it, he was on his knees before her, burying his head in her bosom.

She clung to him as to salvation, then gently raised his head, lowered hers, and their lips met. The intensity of the kiss was overpowering, sprung from the desperate needs inside both of them. They were sealed together almost as one, falling, falling. . . . Suddenly there was a scrape, a harsh laugh from somewhere beyond their own consciousnesses. They pulled apart and looked up to see the captain gripping the edge of the doorway, sweat pouring down his face, with a wicked look in his eyes.

"Pray do not let me interrupt your games." He hacked, then, the cough making his whole body shudder before collapsing in a pile on the floor.

Husband and wife sat stunned for a moment before Keith rose in a rage. "The villain! This is the kind of man I am destined to save! I'll not have it! He goes back into the waves tonight!"

Emily truly believed Keith capable of throwing Jason over the cliffs at that instant. And although the idea had its merits, she soon prevailed upon him to calm down, and between them they carried the captain back to his bed where he lay, to all intents and purposes, unconscious once more. Then she led Keith back to the kitchen.

"Please forgive him, Keith. He was not in his right mind. He is obviously a very sick man."

"Sicker in mind than body, I think," muttered Keith before adding, "and perhaps you'd best put up some coffee."

"Yes," she agreed, disappointment pouring through her, crushing the lovely heightened feeling

74

she'd felt for a few moments. Then she started the coffee while Keith corked the bottle of port and carefully deposited it and its brothers in the pantry.

He poked his head back into the kitchen briefly. "I'd best be off to the tower to light up." And he was gone.

Emily watched his departure, feeling strangely bereft. The captain's shocking behavior had sobered her, as well, and there seemed nothing left to do but prepare some dinner. Maybe it would take her mind off what was obviously now going to be another lonely night. So thinking, she chose some salted cod and soon had fried cod fritters sizzling and leftover baked beans warming. When she heard the captain hacking again, she found half a cup of port remaining on the kitchen table, and took it in to him. The wine seemed to help, and soon he was sleeping again, having uttered not a single word about his recent strange behavior.

Emily completed the cooking preparations, but still Keith did not return. She knew now the length of time required for him to ignite his lamps, and, realizing that he was probably sitting up in the lamp room licking his injured pride, she took his dinner to him. Anything was preferable to eating alone.

Emily slowly negotiated the darkened steps, carefully avoiding the half-dried wash hanging limply in all directions, then quietly poked first the enameled pots of food, then her own head through the trap door. The warmth from the lamps hit her like a wave and, in the great brightness, she was blinded a moment before her eyes adjusted and she was able to pick out her husband's figure gazing through his windows out to sea.

"The wind is down tonight," she commented.

He started, then turned. "Yes, it has become quite calm. The calm before another storm, I think." He came over and helped her up the remaining ladder rungs into the tiny space.

"I had not realized it could become so warm up here," she observed.

"Yes. When the wind ceases, it is quite cozy. Although on a warm summer night, it becomes like an oven—even with the window to the catwalk open."

"But it opens to the landward side. Surely the circulation would improve if it opened to the sea?"

"For the summer, yes. But in winter when I must go out to scrape the ice, the sea wind is strong enough at times to extinguish the lights."

"So everything is designed most thoughtfully."

"Yes. There be reasons for most things in life." He gazed speculatively out to sea.

"Will you have some dinner with me? It is still warm, I think."

"Thank you for the thought. I fear I am accustomed only to solitude, and make poor company."

"I beg to differ with you, husband, but I believe a little readjustment of habits is all that is necessary. All men are social creatures by nature."

"And all women, too? Patience was not."

"If you will forgive my saying it, I believe her sickness was more of the soul than the body, but I know only what I have pieced together from your comments."

"Not all of them charitable, I am afeared. Come, set up against this window and I will try a bite to eat, although I have not much appetite."

Emily pulled spoons and napkins out of her apron

pocket, then watched as he tentatively tasted one of her fritters, then went back for more with apparent relish.

"You have a way with food. I am accustomed to boiled codfish with little variation."

"My mother may be a bit flighty, but she caught and held my father—between voyages, of course— with food. I do believe her fascination with polished floors and furniture, and gossip, of course, is a way of making up for the lack of men around the house. If she'd had some sons to scuff the place a bit, she might be different. But with all that, she is a good and loving woman." Emily thought nostalgically of their last moments together.

"Yes. She produced you, after all. I suspect, though, that you more strongly resemble your oft-absent father."

Emily smiled. "Perhaps. I should like you to meet him someday." She helped herself to a fritter, chewed on it meditatively, then spoke again. "Do you think you could tell me how you came to marry Patience? It might help me if I understood better."

Keith stopped, a spoonful of beans midway to his mouth. "That is long in the past. I fail to see how it could help now."

"To know more about you will help me tremendously. I know you are a very capable person, but still strangely unsure of yourself. Your beginnings account for part of that . . ." She paused while he gagged on the beans. "But that should be well in the past with your age and experience . . ."

"Emily," he interrupted, not unkindly, "I will be thirty-five years of age at my next birthday. Whilst that does give me an advance in years on yourself, I

77

am hardly doddering yet." And almost as a reflex action he popped another fritter into his mouth.

"How did you meet Patience?" she pursued stubbornly.

He sighed. "If you must know. . . ." He stood up then and began to pace the tiny circumference around the blazing light, stooping occasionally to adjust one of the burners for oil flow before continuing. "I was twenty-four, invalided out of the Army after Gettysburg." His pacing slowed, as if finding the reliving of those years a difficult experience. "A commanding officer for whom I had had the opportunity to do a service took kindly to me, and, knowing I had no people, sent me to his own. I recuperated slowly, with his wife and spinster daughter tending all my needs. It was the first time any kindness had been lavished upon me, and, when the officer returned, he suggested the affiliation with his daughter. With gratitude I accepted Patience and her modest dowry. She was considerably older than I, but still within childbearing age, and I had hopes for a family. . . ."

"With the dowry and at their suggestion, I bought into a small dry-goods establishment in their town, and without really the capacity for it, settled down to the life of a burgher."

He was still pacing, but stopped to stuff and light his pipe. "All might have gone moderately well but for the fact that my patron suddenly died, leaving his heartbroken wife to pine away in short order after him. Only then did it come to light that Patience's father—and my hero—had left a sizeable gambling debt behind. There was no choice but to sell my piece of the business and the house to make amends and look about for another means of support. I had always hankered after the sea, but knew I could not in conscience take to it, leaving a totally distraught wife behind—Patience was never able to hold her head up in that town again after the scandal of her much-respected father—so we came here. The Lighthouse Service gave preference to wounded veterans."

He paced some more. "I thought the air and solitude would improve her condition, but the years just slipped her further into herself. I made a poor decision."

Emily, hardly prepared for the nature of his disclosure, found herself letting out her pent-up breath. "Why, Keith—it is just like one of Mr. Dickens's novels!"

He stopped to regard her. "I did not expect you to sneer at me, Emily."

"Oh, please. I am not doing that, husband. It is just that your story is so dramatic, and so sad."

"It is not a story, but my life. A very ill-begotten one, I am afraid."

"There is no need for you to apologize, or be defensive about it. It would appear you acted honorably in all instances."

"Indeed. 'Keith Judson, honorable bastard!' You may have that emblazoned on my tombstone when the time arrives."

"Please!"

"Get you off to bed, now, woman, and leave me to my light and my thoughts."

"Your thoughts, indeed, sir! With all this glorious brightness about you, such thoughts might improve in tone. Patience may not have noticed your black moods, but I do not intend to mope about for ten years with them. This island is not big enough for the weight you insist on carrying about between your shoulders.'' And picking up the now-empty dinner cans, Emily descended to the house below.

She did not see Keith look after her longingly, then bury his head in his hands in despair.

CHAPTER 5

Feb. 8. Morning dawned clear after still night. Temperature improved to 10°. The captain had a relapse yesterday. His total recovery doubtful.

Emily was puttering about the kitchen. Her cold had settled down some, and only an occasional sneeze broke the silence. She'd fed Keith some breakfast, then sent him off to bed for the morning. It had been clear from his tightly drawn face when he brought in Flora's dawn offering that he hadn't napped much in his tower last night. The fact that he'd consented without much fuss had told just how tired he was.

Help me to ease up on my caustic comments, Lord. The poor man's life hasn't exactly been a bed of roses, she offered up. But with her basic common sense, it was still difficult for Emily to accept his recurrent self-recriminations. It had been hard enough for her to get to sleep last night. Finally, she'd relit the lamps and, in a spurt of otherwise useless energy, had finished the rag rug. As it turned out, Patience's taste had run to muted blues and grays, and the final result, a five by seven oval, looked quite pleasant on the kitchen floor in front of the big stove.

Emily eyed the rest of the room critically. Since this was where they spent most of their waking hours, she might as well make it as cozy as possible. With this in mind, she raided the parlor of its gingerbread clock, and set it to ticking atop one of her counters. Then she decided to hang her china plates. She chose the best placement on the wall and attached heavy string in loops through the holes behind the rims, but couldn't wait for Keith to get up to fetch her a hammer and nails. After quickly peeking in at the sleeping captain, she donned her cloak and boots and set off for the tool shed in the barn.

It was the first time Emily had really been out on her own, and the invigorating, frigid air made her feel a bit adventurous. She had a good look at the stock first, giving a few kernels of corn to the hens, then patting Flora for a moment. Emily also paused to admire the barn itself. It was constructed, like the house, out of the rubblestone so readily available on the island. Its walls were more than four feet thick, whitewashed inside and out. It was surprisingly clean and tidy, and warm, too, certainly above freezing. *Must be the thick walls, she thought. A bit less sturdy and the storms that blew up out here should long ago have swept the whole edifice into the sea.* Emily shivered at the thought, then with another few words for the chickens, for which she was rewarded with a still-warm egg, she went into the adjoining toolroom for the hammer and nails.

Armed with these necessaries, she set off again

toward the house, then detoured for a quick view of the mainland. It was a lovely, sunny morning, and for the first time she could make out the lines of the Maine coast clearly. She stood gazing at the mainland a bit wistfully, wishing she'd remembered to bring some of the sweet potatoes from her mother's basement, when she caught sight of a small boat hoisting its single sail at the edge of the ice floe. She watched with interest. It was too early for the fishermen to be out, but who else would brave this very changeable sea in February?

After a few moments, as the speck became larger, it dawned upon her that the boat was making for their island! With some amazement, mixed with trepidation, Emily raced back to the house to wake Keith. Certainly he'd not wish to sleep through an event of this magnitude.

First remembering to leave the hammer and nails with the precious egg in a safe place in the pantry, Emily raced up the stairs and into the bedroom.

"Keith! Keith!"

He sat up with a start, looking very wooly-headed. "What is it? What is the matter?"

Emily tried to calm down. "Nothing, I hope. But there is a small boat making for our island. I thought you would wish to know."

"Is that what all the galloping and dancing about is for? I thought sure it was an earthquake, at the very least."

"Would you rather I had left you to sleep?" she replied a bit testily.

"No. No. Of course not." He raised himself out of bed with an effort and began searching for his boots. "Visitors are almost nonexistent in February. In fact,

83

I can think of no other occasion in all my years here, notwithstanding the arrival of yourself and the captain, of course." He finally found his boots under the bed, and grumbling to himself, pulled them over the trousers he'd neglected to remove for his nap. "Although for a solitary life there's been an exceptional amount of excitement about this establishment of late."

"Would you prefer it otherwise?"

He looked at her with bleary eyes. "No. I suppose I did bring it upon myself." Then, as an afterthought, "I judge there's still time for me to shave. Have you any hot water on the stove?"

"I'll have some ready for you in an instant." And she ran down to the kitchen.

Fifteen minutes later, shaven and with a cup of hot coffee to warm him, Keith looked remarkably well. "All right. I suppose it would be time to head for the harbor. They might need some help in laying by. Do you wish to come along?" He looked at Emily more closely. Her cloak was already about her shoulders. "Yes, I guess you do. You know, for someone who's been on the island less than a week, you seem mighty anxious for company. You really haven't any concept of the loneliness of life out here yet, have you?" Not waiting for an answer, he made for the door, Emily following a bit meekly, like a puppy that had been chastised by its master.

Keith did not offer his arm, but strode on ahead, and soon Emily was again slipping and sliding down the path next to the boat slip on her way to the tiny inlet where they'd found their treasure the day before. Today there was no gift from the sea bobbing among the rocks, but, lifting her head, Emily immediately spied the small craft. Their island was definitely its destination. As it came steadily closer, she made out three figures—all male—none of whom she recognized.

But wait! The one with the reddish beard—could that be Red, one of Jason's men whom she'd viewed stealthily from the wharf last summer? Saying nothing, she stood by her equally silent husband and waited for the boat to maneuver itself within landing distance. Although the craft was quite close, it took three tries and fifteen minutes to navigate the dangerous natural twin rock jetties on either side of the inlet. Finally, one of the men thought to throw a rope to Keith, and after several attempts he caught it cleanly, and helped to guide them to shore. In another moment all three men had jumped ashore, and stood about staring at Keith and Emily. Finally one of them spoke.

"Be you the keeper of the light?"

"I am. And this is my wife. What may we do for you?"

The spokesman, a bit older and more grizzled than the other two, tipped his hat momentarily in Emily's direction before continuing.

"We be from the schooner *Juliana*. I am the first mate, called Pert, and these be Red and Smoot." He pointed in the general direction of the other two. "Our cap'n and bosun set off in a storm five days back, and only one's returned—found drownded up on the harbor beach yestiddy morn. We're seeking to know if you saw any sign of the cap'n. Water currents been crazy with the storms about, and we thought mebbe there was a chance he could've lodged up hereabouts."

"Indeed, I am sorry to hear about your bosun, but

we have good news of the captain. He lies up in the house—sick but alive.''

The sailors silently exchanged expressions of genuine pleasure and relief.

"That be good news, indeed! May we see him?" asked Pert.

"Of course. Come along up, gentlemen, and my wife will give you something to warm you after your cold journey, as well.''

"Many thanks." Pert took a step, then paused as if suddenly remembering something. "Red, fetch that parcel, eh?'' He looked at Emily for a moment. "You be the new wife, I expect. Word about poor Emmett and our search kind of got around town fast, there being nothing else doing these days. Anyhow, your mother sent you a packet on the off chance we'd get this far.''

Emily smiled her delight and without further ado, they all marched single-file up past the boathouse to the cottage. Once inside, Keith showed the men to the sleeping captain, while Emily bustled about the kitchen, putting on a fresh pot of coffee and quickly concocting some cod chowder. Once she'd gotten these underway, she turned her attention to the parcel she'd been itching to open.

Emily carefully undid the layers of sea-splashed newspapers, putting the paper behind the stove to dry. Even if they were not recent issues, Keith would probably still enjoy reading them. For all that, she would probably look at them with more appreciation herself. Next, she carefully rolled up the hemp cord that had held the parcel together and tucked it into her new "whatnot" drawer for future emergencies. Finally she was ready to examine the contents. There was a short note from her mother:

Dearest Emily,

You've been gone but a few days, and already your sisters and I miss your presence. Belinda is now in charge of the pies, and I must say that her crusts do not hold a candle to yours yet. But she sends you one of her efforts with love, anyway.

Your marriage was the talk of the town for three days until the finding of that poor sailor, may he rest in peace. I hope I did the right thing by you, my dear, but you did seem ready to leave the nest.

Good luck to you and love from all of us.

Your affectionate mother,

Prudence Perkins

Emily had to pull out her handkerchief and wipe her eyes before evaluating the offerings before her: a meat pie from her sister, a jug of molasses, several dozen of the coveted sweet potatoes, and a bolt of modest brown wool. She seized upon the cloth and let it fall open. Marvelous! Obviously intended for her as makings for a new dress, it would do instead for a pair of trousers for herself, with plenty enough to spare for a new shirt for Keith. Bless her mother. She'd obviously spent the last of her winter housekeeping money. But Father was due back in the spring, and if his voyage had been successful, Mother's kitty would soon be overflowing again.

With a start, Emily realized that her chowder pot was about to boil over. She ran to tend it, then cleared and set the table for their guests, whose voices had been a low hum in the background. Just as she was about to check on their progress, Keith returned to the kitchen with them. The men sat down to eat, and Emily offered a short grace, then served the meal.

Pert spoke first. "What think you, Red, about the cap'n?"

"He be in no condition to travel yet, calm sea or not."

"I think the same," agreed Pert. "Mr. Judson, be you willing to tend to him awhile longer? We could fetch a doctor, but the seas may not be as agreeable tomorrow and the next day as today."

"I am no expert, sir, but I am unsure how much use a doctor could be at this time. The man mainly needs rest to get over the fever. The frostbite he will have to live with later."

"Aye. So we may leave him with ye?"

"None of us has a choice if we wish your captain to survive. Taking him out on an open boat today would surely be tantamount to murder."

"Aye." Pert spooned up the last of his chowder, then rubbed his bowl clean with a piece of bread. "This be fine chowder, missus."

"Would you like more?"

"Wouldn't say no."

Emily refilled all their bowls while Pert furrowed his brows with thinking. "What say we plan to return for him in a week or so, weather and sea providing?" he looked to Keith for his approval.

"I am quite sure he will be sound enough to travel the distance to the mainland in that time—weather permitting."

"Done, then." Pert finished his second bowl, drained his third cup of coffee, and pushed back his chair preparatory to rising. He looked at Emily. "If you'll be wantin' to write a note to your people,

88

missus, I'll be happy to deliver it. And make up a list of some stores you'd be likin'. We'll bring 'em back for you next trip. Don't be shy with it, now. Least we can do for your savin' the cap'n.'' He stood up. "Take your time, boys. I'll just have another look-see while you finish. We'd best be leavin' within the hour, though, 'fore the tide changes.'' And Pert sauntered across the hall, picking his teeth contentedly with a fish bone.

Emily left the rest of the men to their third helpings and raced around searching for paper and pencil. In the parlor, where she could more easily concentrate, she penned a brief note of thanks, with only a few positive particulars about the events of the past days, to her mother. Then she settled down to concentrate on the list. At the top was "writing paper," then underneath:

— whatever papers, journals, books might be in the
   general store
   (would love something from Mr. Herman Melville or Mr. Charles Dickens.)
—enough bright hanks of wool for two sweaters
—knitting needles, assorted sizes
—flour sifter
—a ham or some smoked bacon
—dried fruit
—a good-sized cheese
—yeast

Her fierce concentration on the list was penetrated by voices from the study beyond the wall. She tried not to eavesdrop, but after a moment couldn't help herself. She put down the pencil she'd been chewing on and listened to the muted bits of conversation between Pert and Captain Cobb.

" . . . cave."

"Didn't make it."

"Cargo?"

"Gone down with Emmett."

"What luck! A wasted voyage, then."

"Not altogether . . . the clean stuff on board will cover our expenses. And"—Jason's voice grew hoarser with effort—"there's still enough in the cave to cover our old age"—he hacked, then continued—"if I should live so long."

"Listen, cap'n. Worry not. Just get better. The boys and I'll work up another plan meantime."

"Good man, Pert—" and Jason went on a coughing jag.

"Enough talk. We'll have to run with the tide now."

Emily quickly added sugar, tea, oatmeal, cornmeal, split peas, barley, and spices to the list and hurried into the kitchen before Pert could notice her absence. There she briefly consulted Keith, who added some foodstuffs for the animals to the list, as well as a few tools. Then he glanced at the list once more before asking a bit wistfully, "Think you it would be overstretching to request an extravagance?"

"What had you in mind, husband?"

"Your cooking has been a wonder, my dear, but I have a strong penchant for pickles."

"Pickles!"

"I've been remembering the pickle barrel in the general store. Haven't had one since summer."

Emily laughed and gave him an affectionate kiss on the cheek. "Of course." And she added at the bottom

90

of the list "pickles and crackers if possible." Then, as an afterthought, she wrote "Thank you," and signed her name, "Emily Judson," for the first time.

At that point Pert came bustling in to collect his men, who were struggling to get their greatcoats on over their thick seamen's sweaters. Stuffing Emily's note and list into his pocket, he made a quaint little thank-you speech for the hospitality, then they were all off, Keith walking with them in case they needed assistance in getting the boat off again.

Emily took a bowl of the chowder broth in to the captain. He was barely able to swallow it before he dozed off again, exhausted by the recent excitement.

After that, instead of immediately clearing up her kitchen, Emily shoved the dirty crockery into a pile, making a clean space on the kitchen table. She'd quite run out of paper with her notes, and regretfully had had to remove the end sheets from one of Keith's books to replenish her supply. But the urge was strong to sketch an idea she'd had, so she set to it, all else far removed from her mind. She was still at it when Keith surprised her sometime later to report the men safely on their way.

"What have you there, Emily?"

A bit guiltily, she started to cover the sheet, then handed it to him.

"I did not know you were an artist."

"I am not. I just have the urge to put things on paper occasionally."

Keith studied the sheet again. "This is a remarkably good likeness of our three recent visitors."

"Actually, I was interested in their sweaters."

"Sweaters?"

"Yes. Did you notice how warm and comfortable

they looked? Particularly with the high rolled collars. I thought to knit one for each of us in that style if they bring back the wool on the list. Then I thought to sketch a likeness before I forgot the stitch styles and texture. The faces quite naturally became attached to their sweaters."

Keith gave it another quizzical look. "And then our kitchen appeared around them, I take it."

"Yes." She looked at him a little self-consciously. "You do not approve?"

"On the contrary. I find it a most marvelous thing. I shall have to find some more paper for you before you destroy my small library." He smiled; then his face became suddenly serious. "I have a bit of spare glass I've saved from the repair of broken tower panes— the birds do insist on flying into them on occasion— and some old wood in my shop. Would you mind if I were to build a frame for it? I've always wanted a few pictures about the house."

"Oh, Keith, you really are serious! No one has taken my sketches to heart before."

"A pity, then."

He carefully rolled up the character study of the three men sitting around their kitchen table and disappeared, leaving Emily to wash the dishes.

The room tidy again, Emily remembered her gift of wool cloth and spread it out on the kitchen table. It wasn't until Emily found it necessary to move her nose closer and closer to the cloth that she realized the winter afternoon was almost gone. She got up to light the lamps, then began preparing a dish of sweet potatoes with molasses for their dinner. She had just slipped it into the oven when she heard the cottage door open and slam shut, and glanced around in time to see Keith hastening toward his tower with some sort of parcel tucked under his arm. She started to greet him, but he was already gone, his footsteps lightly echoing up the tower stairs.

Emily shrugged to herself, then cleared the table of the sewing and went to fetch the last piece of smoked ham from the pantry. As she sliced it for the frying pan, she began to hope fervently that the captain's men were serious about the gift provisions. Combining Jason's increasing appetite and Keith's and her own healthy ones would soon leave the larder bare—if, of course, one discounted the seemingly endless supply of flour and salted cod. And her sister's pie, of course. Emily was saving that for the morrow.

She paused in her labors and went now across the hall to stand in the doorway and observe him. His breathing was heavy and labored, with much wheezing. *Probably a touch of pneumonia. And no wonder. But one day soon he will be well enough to get about. And if that happens before the return of his sailors, God help us all.*

Thus musing, Emily was startled by Keith's sudden hand on her shoulder.

"Emily!"

"What?" She followed him into the kitchen. "What is it, Keith?"

"I would like to know your recent thoughts whilst standing there. I called your name twice from the hall to no avail."

"I was just listening to the captain's breathing, worrying if he has a chance with the pneumonia that seems to be settling in." And she blushed slightly at the thought of what she hadn't said. Keith was quick to notice.

93

"Then why the rising color in your cheeks, my girl? Thus far you have completely avoided telling me how well you knew the captain, and when."

These were fighting words, and Emily rose to the bait. "Keith Judson! If you refuse to stop this ridiculous jealousy, it will be impossible to live around here, and I shall be forced to return to the mainland with Jason's sailors!" Once said, Emily wanted to bite her tongue, but it was too late.

"Aha! So now it is not 'the captain,' but 'Jason,' is it?"

"Yes, Jason it is!" she flaunted. "The same Jason who flirted with an innocent small-town girl last summer. And that girl is still innocent, no thanks to you!" And Emily stomped out of the kitchen, throwing over her shoulder as she left, "And both of you he-men can eat your supper tonight without me!" Emily ignored the very un-Keithlike oaths emanating from the kitchen and continued up the stairs to the bedroom where she swathed herself in a bundle of quilts and lay in the gloom until she fell asleep.

Sometime later she felt herself being shaken roughly awake.

"Emily, Emily!" It was Keith's voice, insistent.

"Go away," she muttered and buried her head under her pillow.

The pillow was pried loose. "Emily! The captain is breathing very badly. I fear he may stop completely. I do not know what to do next. I need your help."

That woke her up. She sat up quickly. "Yes, of course, Keith. I am coming."

She untangled herself from the bedclothes and jumped to the floor, still fully clothed, then followed the already disappearing candle flame down the steps.

The kitchen and study were both blazing with light and heat, and Emily realized with a guilty start that Keith must have been nursing Jason for some hours. The captain was propped upright on his pillows, almost purple for want of oxygen. Emily gasped involuntarily, then turned to Keith.

"Have you any camphor?"

"Yes, some left over from Patience."

"Get it quickly, please, while I boil some water."

Within a few minutes, after uttering a few pleas to the Lord for guidance, Emily had a boiling kettle lodged almost next to Jason's mouth, the camphorated steam inside wafting into his nose and throat. Through the night and into the early morning hours, more water was boiled; the kettle, constantly refilled; the patient's back, massaged, in an attempt to break up the dreadful congestion. Light was beginning to creep through the shutter cracks when Jason, unconscious throughout the ordeal, began to breathe more easily, then drifted into sleep.

Emily sat back in her chair with a sigh, and reached behind her for Keith's hand. He had taken only brief breaks from running, fetching, assisting, to race up to the tower and tend his light. She turned her head to look at his weary face.

"Thank you, husband. For someone who professes to hate the man, you tended our captain exceptionally well."

He gave her a small smile. "Forgive me for things I have said in anger, Emily. Like the man or not, I'll have neither the sea nor the sickness take him. I want him out of here in one piece so there'll be no more regrets. You forget I saw Patience go of the same thing. But 'our captain,' as you put it, is made of

95

sterner stuff. Through it all I sensed a willingness for life, not the defeat of Patience. This I must admire." He was silent for a moment, then added, "I am quite sure that now he is over the worst. It was such a night that took Patience."

"I am sorry."

"I've put the matter behind me. I think now that I did my best. Patience, as usual, was not willing to do hers."

Emily could see a kind of exhilaration behind Keith's exhaustion. Perhaps the captain's illness had finally given him the catharsis he'd needed. Emily fervently prayed that this was the case.

"You are exhausted, husband. You've had little sleep for several days. Close your lights and tend to Flora, then go to sleep. I will stay here and keep watch."

"You are tired, too."

"No. Well, a little. But I had several hours of sleep before you woke me. I will be fine. Please."

"You are probably right. It won't do for all of us to be sick." And with a gentle touch of his fingertips to her cheek, he was off.

CHAPTER 6

Feb. 9. Weather holding still, clear, and cold. Had visit from crew of Juliana *yesterday after which captain survived night of crisis with pneumonia.*

A croaking sound woke Emily from her doze. She stirred in her rocking chair by the sickbed, feeling slightly chilled. She opened her eyes to see Jason awake and aware, the fever gone from his eyes. The croaking came again. He was trying to say something. She raised him on his pillows a moment, watched his lips. "Drink," he was trying to say. He was thirsty!

Emily smiled with relief, patted the damp curls away from his eyes, and creaked out of the chair to find something appropriate. In a few minutes she was back with a hot toddy of the port wine, warmed in a little water with cloves and sugar. He took the spoonfuls gratefully until the cup was empty and color began returning to his face, although it was hard to tell about his color, with all that great soft beard. Emily

97

smiled again at the thought, then gently wiped his mouth.

"You are quite awake now, aren't you?"

He croaked a yes in reply.

"Please. Do not try to talk. You are not yet strong enough. But you do not wish to sleep again?"

He shook his head.

"Fine. Then I must entertain you. Would you like me to continue the story Keith was reading the other night?"

He looked confused for a moment, trying to remember.

"Never mind. It was a good sea story, *Moby Dick*, about men off to hunt for whales."

Recognition returning to his eyes, he struggled to say yes.

"Hush. Enough. I will read where we left off." Emily got up and found the book on the shelves, resettled herself, and began. It was some time later, when the insanity of Captain Ahab began to assert itself that Emily found her voice tiring, paused, and looked up to find Keith in the doorway.

"Husband! You should be sleeping!"

"That I was, and for some time. It is already late afternoon, Emily."

"It must have been the story. The time passed quickly."

"You have a lovely reading voice. I had thought this story fit only for a male reading, but you bring new insights to it."

Emily blushed and rose. "It will be time to see about some nourishment for all of us." And she escaped past her husband and his eyes full of longing and admiration into the kitchen.

After putting the meat pie into the oven, Emily beat up their current stock of two eggs with some cream and scrambled them soft, in butter, for Jason. With the addition of another cup of port toddy, his dinner was complete, and Emily took it across the hall and slowly administered it.

Keith had disappeared again, but soon returned with a slamming and clanking from outside. *Must be another bucket of milk,* thought Emily. *I'll try to make a batch of soft-curd cheese from it. There really is too much to drink.* So thinking, she brought her mind back to her patient, who was opening his mouth to her automatic shoveling motions. *Whoops.* She'd have to improve her aim. The last spoonful of egg missed its mark completely.

"I am sorry," she apologized with a smile. "My mind was elsewhere. No, do not try to answer me yet, please. Tomorrow will be soon enough. We ought to try to get you out of bed for a few minutes tomorrow, too. Can't have you looking like a weakling when your men return!"

Jason gave her a wan smile, finished his meal, then drifted gratefully off to sleep again. Emily left him well propped up, then surveyed him with a critical nurse's eye. *Hopefully he will have a better night. We can all use the rest.* She banked the fire, lowered the flame in the oil lamp on the desk, and returned to the kitchen. Keith was sitting next to the table, smoking his pipe and whittling at a long piece of driftwood.

"What are you working at?"

"A crutch for the captain. He is weak now, but when he first tries to stand, his frostbitten feet will be giving him some trouble. Hope you don't mind the wood shavings. I'll be cleaning them up."

99

Emily smiled. "Please don't worry about a little mess. I am happy enough to have some company here."

"I had hoped so," he muttered, then as if that were too much of a revelation, he retreated back to his silence.

Emily, satisfied with his presence and the soft scraping sounds, set about separating the milk for her anticipated cheese, all the while keeping an eye on her pie in the oven. As an afterthought, she boiled a little more water and made another cup of hot toddy, presenting it to Keith with a little flourish.

He sniffed at it with amusement.

"And what is this?"

"Something to fend off the cold and the captain's germs." She sat down for a moment, and watched him sip from the cup appreciatively.

"Surely your temperate mother did not teach you to make a hot toddy?"

"Definitely not. Sometimes I think I may have hidden talents."

He set down his now empty pipe. "Undoubtedly. And it will be a mighty pleasure seeking them out at leisure,"—he paused—"assuming, of course, you have the fortitude to give me and the island another chance."

Emily felt a twinge of guilt. "Oh, Keith, we have both said things in anger that were better left unsaid. I am not one to give up easily, especially with marriage. Yet it seems to me that something is missing. I begin to feel companionable with you, but some need inside me is crying out to be filled."

"Yes, at least you are honest about it. Patience never could bring herself to talk it out. Her needs were the opposite—an aversion, if you will, to men. Some women are better off left as spinsters." He stopped, suddenly realizing. "Forgive me, I had meant not to speak of her again."

"No matter. I am used to it already, anyway. It's not possible for you to completely block out all those years of your life. And probably not healthy, either."

"You are an amazing woman, Emily—and a tempting one," he whispered gruffly.

He looked at her, and with a slow smile began to rise from his chair, his toddy forgotten for the moment. Gently his arms encircled Emily's shoulders and he began to draw her toward him. Brown eyes stared longingly into blue ones, as his lips drew nearer and gently settled on hers. He gathered her softness against his muscular chest. Emily began to tremble. Then she panicked and cried, "Dinner! I'll not have another ruined meal. Besides, I've eaten nothing since yesterday noon. And you will need to light your lights before nightfall."

He smote his forehead with the palm of his hand. "You will be the cause of my professional ruination, woman! Never has the light been farther from my mind." And he laid down his knife and stick and hastened out.

Emily grinned a little grin to herself as she cleaned up the mess and set the table. Keith certainly was slower in getting to the romantic point at issue than the volatile Jason, but then Keith had been burned too many times. His shyness was endearing, so long as one knew there was definitely a fire burning there. She tingled in anticipation as she set out the pie.

Keith returned in a few minutes, looking worried. "What's the matter?"

"There is a heavy fog beginning to roll in, and the wind has freshened considerably. I fear we're in for more bad weather." He looked at the dinner longingly. "Just one bite, then, and I must go out and wind up the fog bells."

He barely sat down, wolfed a huge piece of hot pie, then was off and running to the hall for his outdoor clothes which hung on pegs there. Emily followed him with a lantern.

"Will you need this to see?"

"No. I could find my way around here blind." Then he was gone, the door behind him almost swinging off its hinges with a sudden gust of wind.

Emily returned to her dinner and waited, her ears straining for the sounds of the telltale bells that would signal his return. For a while she heard only the rising wind, buffeting the house. Suddenly, they began: deep, resonant, steady. The peals sounded every ten seconds. With a sigh, she resumed eating her dinner. He should be back momentarily. But five minutes passed, then ten, and he did not return. Emily kept consulting the clock on the counter as if her mind were playing tricks. No. It was a full twenty minutes now—time enough for him to have checked the livestock and return. Finally, unable to stand the suspense any longer, Emily took the lantern, donned her cloak, and went out into the night.

The door slammed behind her, and she looked about in surprise. A different world greeted her. Swirls of fog were blowing in every direction, along with stinging pellets of ice. It was impossible to see more than three feet in any direction. Using the bells as a guide, she attempted to hold her cloak about her, while carrying the lantern. After a few steps, however, the wind extinguished the light, then pulled the lantern itself from her hand. In dismay, she heard it clattering away over the rocks. Bent over with the hurricane force, she paused, wondering now how to return to the house herself. She determined to take ten more paces forward before making a decision. On the seventh step her foot struck something soft. It was Keith, lying unconscious, his face and hands already turning icy.

"Keith! Keith!"

Useless. She had to get him back to the house. And there was no one to help. No one but herself and God. "Please, Lord," she begged aloud into the wind, "Give me strength. Please show me the way back." And suddenly the low keening of the wind changed. She could almost make out the sound of her name. "Emily," it whispered. "Emily."

Following the sound, she managed to drag Keith by the arms for what seemed an interminable period before backing straight into something solid. Emily dropped her burden for a moment to feel the object. It was the strong stone wall of the cottage!

Giving silent thanks for God's answer to her desperate plea for help, she again picked up Keith's arms and edged around the wall until she felt the smoothness of the wooden door. Leaning hard against it, she pulled Keith through the opening, slammed the door, then collapsed in a heap beside him.

After a long, winded minute, Emily got up and hauled Keith into the kitchen by the fire. There she began a repetition of the morning they'd found Jason, seemingly a year ago. Remove the sodden clothes, check for frostbite. What had happened? The answer came soon enough. He had a great swollen gash on his forehead. Something had hit him with a strong enough blow to knock him unconscious. Emily ran upstairs for bedding and pillows and made him as comfortable as possible. Keith was otherwise strong and healthy. She'd just have to wait till he woke up.

In retrospect, it would not be one of Emily's most pleasant memories. Anticipating connubial bliss at last, she found herself, instead, running between two invalids and a lighthouse. Keith had not formally instructed her on the operation of the light, but she had watched him with some attention. After closely examining the lantern, she carried down to the kitchen a well-thumbed book entitled *Instructions and Directions to Lightkeepers*. Between her nursing duties Emily quickly skipped past the first, and most obvious instruction:

> The lighthouse shall be lighted daily, and the lights exhibited for the benefit of mariners, *punctually at sunset*.

Then she arrived at the more complicated part:

> Lighthouse lights are to be kept burning brightly, free from smoke, and at their greatest attainable heights, during each entire night, from sunset to sunrise. The height of the flame must be frequently measured during each watch at night, by the scale graduated by inches and tenths of an inch, with which keepers are provided.

Emily groaned to herself. Keith's scale must be lying about in the tower somewhere. She'd just have to locate it, and do her best. She quickly glanced through the index to see what further information she might glean on the subject, and found instructions for cleaning, placing, removing, and preserving the lamp chimneys; for cleaning the lamps; for keeping the lantern free from ice and snow; for using two or three dozen tools; for preserving and economically using the oil, filling the lamp, using the damper; for precautions against fire; and for dozens of other details of the lightkeeper's daily duties. And she'd thought it was just a matter of turning the light on and off.

Emily pulled distractedly at loose wisps of hair, then took another look at her husband lying helpless by the warmth of the stove. He'd had years of experience. Would she be able to keep this entire ménage going until he recuperated?

Lord, this is Emily again, she pleaded silently. *I am definitely going to need more help, please.*

Gathering her resolve, she slammed the book shut and headed for another investigation of the tower and its mysteries. She had no choice. She would have to do it.

The light did keep functioning, although Emily could not imagine its penetrating the incredible storm. It became a matter of principle. And when the dawn came with no cessation of the heavy weather and its howling winds, she extinguished the light gratefully, returned to the kitchen and a breakfast of cold pie, and fell into an exhausted slumber in a chair next to the stove and the supine Keith.

The next three days were supreme torture. Keith lay in an unseeing stupor, and Jason mended slowly. The storm continued without abatement. Emily grabbed snatches of sleep between now very verbal discussions with God and tending the light, the men, and the livestock. After her second dash out to the barn to milk Flora, Emily found the cow's eyes so

105

mournful and lonely looking that she broke into her first tears, then sobs, all the while hugging the great warm beast till Flora, in sympathy, or perhaps just bemused, began to moo disconsolately.

"There, there, Flora," soothed Emily. "It's going to be all right. Everything is going to be all right." She patted the long brown flanks, then found a brush and began to curry the creature: Long strokes, up and down, all over Flora's body. Flora, unused to such luxurious treatment, mooed again, this time with a change in her voice.

"I never would have believed it possible for a cow to moo with delight, but I do believe you are doing so, my dear," crooned Emily, continuing with the brush. "And you are not to worry. Spring will be here soon and you can go cavorting about the island again. Keith will be better soon, too. Oh, dear! Very soon, I hope." The tears were starting again. It wouldn't do. There was still too much work undone. She could not allow herself to wallow in self-pity. Emily stopped her brushing and stepped back to see the results.

"And very attractive you look, too, lovely Flora. A bit more oats in your hay and you'd be fit for the county fair. But I've really overstayed my visit with you, Flora. I will just attend to your friends, the chickens, and then be off. Duty calls."

And so it went. The lights went on and off per schedule, but only once did she attempt to go out and rewind the bells. It was midday, and she could not find the tower! Suddenly realizing that the entire wooden structure had been blown away, she returned to the house, attempting to convince herself that those crazy enough to be on the sea in such weather deserved what was coming to them.

On the fourth morning, Jason picked up the crutch that Emily had laid by his bed and hobbled into the kitchen where he sank into a kitchen chair gratefully, wiped the sweat of effort from his brow, and inspected the scene. Emily's physical and mental exhaustion was more than evident.

"Emily, you are to go up to your bed in one moment. But first, kindly bring me a bottle of Keith's port," he spoke in a gruff whisper.

In a daze, Emily obeyed. She watched while he pulled the cork and beckoned to her.

"Here. Take a long swallow. That's an order, now."

She did as told.

"Now march upstairs. Get into your bed and sleep. It is my turn to keep watch over your husband."

"But . . ."

"No buts about it. I am stronger today and have nothing better to do. I will call if any problem arises."

Emily had no idea of the time when the slow creak of the stairs woke her from her dead sleep. *Keith!* she thought to herself. *He's better, thank God.* She lay still, her muscles unwilling to move, while the steps came closer. In another moment she saw a tall form enter the door through the twilight of the room. A few more steps and the weary form sank into a sitting position on the bed next to her.

"Keith! I am so happy you are well again," she murmured.

"It is not Keith, but Jason. I tried to rouse you from the foot of the stairs, but my voice was not strong enough to carry—" he took quick, shallow breaths in an effort to refill his obviously tortured lungs. "Your husband has begun to stir, and night is quickly arriving. I cannot manage the tower steps for the light.''

Emily was instantly alert and up. ''You said he is stirring?''

''Yes . . . but the light. . . .''

''You shall not attempt the steps again in your condition. I feel more rested now and will see to everything.'' Gently, she eased Jason down onto the bed as his racking cough began again. ''Stay here until I come for you.''

He did not protest, but docilely allowed her to pull a quilt over his body.

Without a second thought, Emily left Jason in her bed and bounded off to tend the light. If Keith was regaining consciousness, she had no doubt that his first concern would be its maintenance. At least she would be able to reassure him on that point. A half hour later, the chore completed, she arrived in the kitchen to tend to Keith. A quick inspection showed him seemingly asleep, so Emily raced out to the barn to milk Flora, who was lowing in some pain.

''I'm sorry, old girl,'' murmured Emily softly as she began to relieve the cow's swollen udders. ''I did not mean to neglect you, but it couldn't be helped.''

Flora gave Emily a baleful look, but as the pressure eased, she turned to give Emily's face a very wet kiss with her sandpapery tongue.

Emily rubbed the wet spot on the shoulder of her cloak. ''That will be quite enough forgiveness, thank you.'' Emily then removed the milk beyond kicking distance and scattered some grain for the equally annoyed chickens, several of which had already been so bold as to rush up and peck at her skirts while she was tending the cow. She waited a few minutes while the animals scrabbled for their meals, then picked up the lantern preparatory to leaving them in the evening's darkness.

"All right, friends, you may settle down for the night now. Hopefully tomorrow will be a better day." Feeling somewhat cheered by this contact with the living—such as they were—Emily returned to the kitchen. There she was shocked by what she saw. Her husband was sitting bolt upright at the kitchen table, apparently once more in control of his faculties.

"Oh, Keith!" Emily set the milk bucket down with a splash and rushed to his side. "Darling! Thank God you are better!" About to fall into his arms, she was brought stock still within a few inches of her destination by his stony look. Her outstretched arms fell to her sides.

"Whatever is the matter? Are you all right?"

"How long have I been ill?" he asked in a flat voice.

"Almost four days now, but. . . ."

"Presumably you did not expect my recovery. But you could at least have had the decency to wait."

"Whatever are you talking about?"

"Before taking the captain to our bed." The statement was entirely devoid of emotion.

"Your fever must be up. Let me feel your head. I fear you are not completely in your senses yet." She put out her hand tentatively to feel his brow. He slapped it away with some force.

Emily stared, bewildered.

"The captain. He is in our bed, is he not?"

"Good heavens!" Suddenly Emily remembered. "Yes, but. . . ." His meaning dawned with startling clarity. For four days I have done nothing but worry

109

over you and the sick captain, tend your light and livestock, and try to keep us all alive during the worst storm I have ever lived through. With all that, do you seriously think that I had time to even consider a dalliance? Not to mention my marriage vow. As for the captain in our bed—yes, it is true enough. I put him there. For today I slept for the first time in four days, slept like the dead, and Jason had the decency to watch over you during this time. He came to get me when you began to stir. The climbing of those short steps so sapped his strength that I insisted he stay there—in our bed. I had not the strength to carry him back down again." Suddenly winded, Emily sat down across the table from her husband, put her head in her arms, and began to sob uncontrollably, letting out all tensions of the past ordeal. Keith just sat and stared, saying nothing, his face an immobile mask. Then he rose and began to make a pot of coffee.

With the sound of a coffee cup being plunked down in front of her, Emily slowly raised her eyes from her arms to the man seated across the table. She spoke to him in a calm, conversational tone.

"After I get a night's sleep, I will repack my trunk. The captain's men will come eventually, now that the storm has passed. If there is time before they arrive, I will finish the new wool shirt I've been making for you. You have need for another one. The elbows are almost worn through on your two others." She rose as if the subject were closed and automatically began to tidy up the kitchen. As an afterthought, she added, "We may as well allow the captain to remain upstairs. Neither of us has the energy to remove him tonight. I will sleep in the study." And she began to walk out of the kitchen.

"Wait." The hard edge of his voice stopped her in the doorway. "Where will you go?"

"Home, at first, but not for long. I believe I can borrow enough money from my mother to get to Bath to take a train to Boston. I should be able to find work there. The inevitable gossip will not allow me to stay in East Egg with any peace of mind. Besides, I should very much like to see a real city." She paused. "I've never really been anywhere but East Egg . . . and here."

"What kind of work can you find? You have no training."

"I can hire out as a domestic. I have lots of experience there," she said rather pointedly. Then she added, "If nothing else, it will give me bed and board and an afternoon off each week. That will be more time to myself than I have ever known."

"You would be wasted as a domestic." His voice was still strong, but beginning to break. "You have greater talents."

"It would seem not. I have failed here, have I not?" And without waiting for a further answer, Emily escaped from the kitchen.

In the study she first closed the door, quietly but firmly. Then she stripped Jason's cot, leaving on it only a quilt with which to cover herself.

With her bravado spent, Emily sat dispiritedly on the edge of the bed. Spying the Bible on the table nearby, she picked it up and thumbed through its pages. *Mother told me there were answers here*, she thought. *I wonder if there could possibly be an answer to my present dilemma.*

She allowed her eyes to skim the print:

. . . Some seeds fell by the wayside . . . Some fell upon stony places, . . . and forthwith they sprung up, . . . and because they had no root, they withered away. . . . But other fell into good ground, and brought forth fruit, . . . but he that received seed into the good ground is he that heareth the word, and understandeth it. . . .

She mused over the words. At times her husband's heart was as rockbound and hard as the Maine coastline. How could he accept God's love if he doubted hers? But if she persevered, just as Keith had persevered in tending the little fir and apple seedlings on his island, perhaps her growing love for him—and God's—would take root and thrive.

Or was it too late? She could see no future in a loveless marriage to a husband sick with unwarranted jealousy. She knew she was strong, but knew also that even the strength of her relationship with God combined with the resiliency of her youth could not help her survive forever on this isolated island with only a man like that for company. She would break like Patience, sooner than Patience, having the intelligence to see her position all too clearly.

CHAPTER 7

Feb. 14. Terrible four-day storm, with gale winds from every direction of the compass finally abated yesterday eve. Bell tower swept into sea, along with outhouse. Livestock survived. Keeper injured, but wife performed all duties relating to light.

Emily was completing preparations for a breakfast of cornmeal mush when she heard the staircase creaking. She turned to find Jason carefully negotiating himself through the kitchen door. He propped his crutch against one wall, then sat at the table with a sigh.

"Good morning," she smiled. "You are looking considerably better."

"Thank you. I could say the same for yourself, if it is allowed." His voice was better, the croak gone.

Emily smiled again. "Yes." She had awakened early with her mind settled into its new course. Then she'd given herself the luxury of a refreshing bath, scrubbed her long hair till it shone, brushed it dry in front of the fire, and had gotten into her second-best dress, a bright blue with crimson trim which set off her coloring. She was determined to be as cheerful as possible for her remaining time on the island.

"Do you feel up to a normal breakfast?"

"I feel like I could eat a whale."

"Sorry, but this will have to do." She set out two plates of the mush, with butter, cream, and molasses for garnish, put the coffeepot on the table, and sat down to join him.

"Should we not wait for your husband?"

Emily colored slightly. "I am not sure of his schedule this morning. I think it best we begin without him."

"As you wish." And without further ado, Jason launched into his breakfast with fervor.

Emily watched him with interest before beginning herself. "I must say, you seem amazingly improved."

"Probably the night in your bed," he grinned, then saw the look in her face. "Sorry. There was trouble about that, then?"

Emily only nodded, then averted her face from his too-speculative look.

"Bad trouble, eh?"

"You might say so." She toyed with her mush for a few moments before asking tentatively, "Do you think there will be room on the small boat for another passenger?"

He stopped eating and looked at her. "Yourself?"

"Yes."

A smile crept slowly into his eyes. "May I presume to think that you are considering leaving him?"

Her eyes were still downcast. "Yes."

"How long have you been married?"

"I am not quite sure . . . The period has been filled with such crises. We married the afternoon before we found you."

He put down his spoon and let out a slow whistle. "I had thought it much longer. You looked so . . . companionable together." He thought a bit. "My rescue was not exactly fortuitous for either of you, then."

She smiled slightly. "I am quite sure you had not planned your shipwreck on my account."

"Too true, my dear. But then, it might have been worth it at that." He picked up his spoon again. "My timing has been rather bad in our brief acquaintance . . . But maybe not so bad, at that." He finished his bowl, then looked her over again. "It has given me the opportunity to observe you on a daily basis, and I very much like what I have seen."

"But you have been unconscious with the fever most of the time," she protested mildly.

"Not so far gone as you might have been led to believe, Emily." He pointed to his bowl. "Is there more where this came from? It is warming me nicely."

"Yes, of course." She rose to refill the bowl and place it again in front of him. That done, she dallied for a moment, then returned to her place.

"If you still have a hankering to see the world, I could take you." He paused in remembrance, his eyes aglow with the vision. "Sun-filled, sandy beaches with palm trees waving, perhaps down Haiti way. And the heat! Warmth, Emily, that you have never known in these godforsaken climes." He glanced involuntarily out the kitchen window and shuddered, then returned to the vision in his head. "And the flowers! Such an exotic profusion you would not believe! The people sing, too, while they work in their boats or the fields. There is a joy of life there which is sadly absent from this dour latitude." Jason looked directly at and through Emily, returning again to his romantic daydreams. "And when we have tired of the heat, off we could go to Europe—London . . . Paris . . . Rome. I could show you the cathedrals, the pictures in the Louvre, and when we grew tired of such things, we could sail through the Mediterranean to older civilizations, stopping for the Parthenon in Greece . . . then down to Egypt to ride the camels and climb the Great Pyramids! Emily, do come with me! The captain's quarters on my boat are well-appointed, but a woman's touch would not be amiss."

Emily just stared at him in slight shock, his beautiful images quickly receding. "And in what capacity would I go? As your mistress? I am married, after all."

Jason merely shrugged. "There are worse things. Like your present plight, it would seem." Ignoring her look of dismay, he dug into his food again with relish, pleased with himself at his proposition, and sure of her obvious acceptance.

"Thank you for the offer, but no. I would merely be taking on another form of imprisonment. Even when we reached a port, you could not introduce me into polite company." She rose. "I shall manage on my own—with God's help," she added with a tilt of her firm chin.

His eyes rose with her and he grinned. "You are really quite beautiful when stubborn and proud. I, for one, should not be ashamed to introduce you as my consort. Just think of it. The boat has not, after all, come for me yet."

Emily left the room, his sardonic smile boring into her back all the way.

Wrapping herself in a huge apron, Emily tied a cap over her clean hair, and spent the morning collecting and sorting out the wash which had finally dried in the tower well, and changing the bed linens. Then she took a wooden bucket full of water and hard lye soap and scrub brush and began to clean, starting with the master bedroom. *At least I can leave Keith with a shipshape house,* she thought to herself, with just the smallest twinge of conscience. When she worked her way into the tiny second bedroom, she almost cried. *What a perfect nursery it would have been!* She sat back on her haunches from her floor-scrubbing labors and gazed around. Those dormer windows under the eaves faced east. The room would be filled with sunshine on a summer's morning. Keith could have made a cradle, and then a crib as the child grew larger . . . With some colorful paint she could have made a wonderful mural on the wall with bright animals and sea creatures to catch the child's fancy . . . She sat there, imagining it in her mind's eye, oblivious to the now real tears trickling down her face. She did not hear the soft footsteps behind her.

"It was once a nursery, and could have been again."

Emily turned. Her husband was standing there, looking gray and worn.

"It is too late. You are incapable of giving me a chance."

Then he, too, was down on his knees, wiping her tear-stained face. "The boat has not come yet. And

117

. . . and I have been sick, and a fool." The words came out harshly, a trial for him to say.

"You have asked for forgiveness before. How am I to believe you this time?"

He held her face between his hands. "I am what I am, Emily. A poor, weak man. For all that, I know now that I love you. Last night was the worst of my life, pacing around the light, knowing I was soon to lose the only real brightness that had ever entered that life—a light that far surpasses that which I tend each night. . . . Please, I beg of you. Give me another chance."

Emily looked into his tortured face, his whole being crying out from his eyes. There was no scorn there, only a pleading from the very depths of his soul.

"You need me." A simple statement.

"Yes, I need you, Emily. As I have never needed anyone in my life. Nor have I ever asked for help. But I ask you now. Stay."

"Take me then, please. Take me now."

She felt her heart pounding in her ears as he gently removed the scrub brush from her hand. When he lifted her bodily, she could feel the pulse beat in his strong arms. In a moment they were across the hall and he was kicking shut their bedroom door.

The late morning sun streamed into the room as he stood with her before the bed, plucked off her cap and apron, and with fingers fumbling, began to unfasten her buttons.

Then he put his hand to hers and held it there a moment before releasing it to gently pull the pins from her hair. Soon the sunshine was heightening the golden glints of her tresses as they spread over her shoulders.

118

He kissed her gently, then held her away from him.

"You are beautiful, Emily."

"You are beautiful, too, husband."

"I thought that a word only for women."

"No."

"I need you now, Emily, my love."

Emily stood before the mirror above the bedroom dresser, marveling at her new body. Her husband lay on the bed, admiring her.

"I feel as if I could stand in for your light tonight," she said. "I feel bright enough to illuminate the entire sea. I had no idea how beautiful it would be."

"Nor I," he smiled.

She knew it was true. It was enough.

Emily hummed to herself as she set about preparing dinner. Gone were the fancy dress and corset. She was again in trousers and an emerald-green shirtwaist blouse with a bright piece of Chinese silk from her trousseau chest tied cheerfully around her neck. In between tending the pots she remembered her Chinese plates, and fetched the hammer and nails long since abandoned on a pantry shelf. After the first round of bangs, the study door across the hall opened and a muzzy-looking Jason emerged, leaning heavily on his crutch.

"What! Is it thundering in February?"

She stopped a moment to nod at him, then removed a nail from between her lips before speaking. "Had a nice nap, Jason?"

"There was little enough else to do," he grumbled. "Everyone just disappeared."

"Fine," she said cheerfully, hanging the first plate

and adjusting it for levelness. "You need all the rest you can get."

"And what are you so all-fired happy about? At breakfast you were in the depths of despair."

"None of your business, sir," she said, returning her face towards the wall so that her rising blush would remain unseen.

He stood wobbling for a moment, then went to sit in the rocking chair by the fire, the better to observe her. "So," he said at last. "The lovebirds have made up."

Emily studiously ignored this comment and proceeded to hammer in the next nail with more flourish than was entirely necessary.

"I take it, then—" he had to raise his voice to be heard above the din she was making—"I take it, then, that I should not be expecting the pleasure of your company for the return trip to the mainland."

She stopped to flash him a sweet smile. "I expect an experienced captain like yourself should be able to survive the three-mile trip with only the companionship of your fellow sailors."

Jason grumped audibly, then lapsed into silence. Emily ignored him, focusing all of her attention on the five plates now hanging in two rows on the wall. She stood back a moment to observe them with a critical eye, then moved to adjust several for balance.

Satisfied at last, she hummed her way to the stove and began to inspect the dinner progress, disregarding Jason's proximity completely. The left-over mush from breakfast was caking nicely in a pan in the oven. And she was experimenting with a codfish bisque. Emily raised a spoonful to her lips to taste it, then wrinkled her nose and added another pinch of salt and a dollop of cream. There seemed to be no getting around codfish. What she should have ordered from the mainland was a cookbook—preferably one titled *A Thousand and One Ways to Prepare Codfish*. If there wasn't such a volume, there ought to be. She smiled to herself.

"Whatever is so amusing?"

"Codfish, of course. I wish a whale would beach up on the shore, or something. Anything for a change from cod every day."

"Wrong season."

"What?" She had the oven door open again.

"I said you'll not find any whales about here in February. A few schools of humpbacks in late summer, perhaps, but that is all."

"Perhaps not."

Jason and Emily both turned at the sound of Keith's voice from the doorway.

"I've seen some schools swim through as late as Thanksgiving. And a few years back, in December, the inspector from the visiting tender told me he'd just passed about a hundred beached up on the shoals down Nantucket way."

"Do come in, Keith," beamed Emily. "Is everything fine in your tower?"

"Yes. It is an exceptionally clear night. I've had the telescope out of its case, and the stars seem very near. Perhaps you would care to observe them with me after supper?"

"I would like nothing better." Their eyes locked and only Jason's grumbling efforts to get up from the rocking chair pulled them apart.

"Here, let me help you," offered Emily.

"No. Allow me," Keith smiled, advancing.

"I thank you both, but I shall do it myself." And

with some effort Jason raised himself. "I think I shall opt for the straight-backed chairs around the table in the future." And he resettled himself with a sigh.

Emily and Keith's eyes met in mutual amusement. The captain was obviously not coping well with their newfound bliss.

Ignoring Jason's discomfiture, Emily showed off her new wall arrangement to Keith, who looked suitably pleased. Then he excused himself a moment, and Emily set the table around Jason, filled the milk jug, and sliced a loaf of bread. The latter was going a bit stale, so she toasted it with lard, then cut it into croutons for the soup bowls. By the time these preparations were completed, Keith had returned with a parcel under his arm. He handed it to Emily.

"I was saving it for an occasion," he smiled again, " but tonight seems as good as any."

Emily unwrapped the old newspapers, revealing her sketch of Jason's men beautifully framed in bits of polished oak.

"Goodness! What a lovely job you have done. It makes my drawing seem quite professional."

"As it is," beamed Keith.

"May I see it?" asked Jason. He carefully inspected the figures before handing it back. "A good likeness."

Emily was surveying the kitchen walls. "What do you think, Keith? On the wall next to the stove, over the dry sink?"

"Perfect." He took the hammer and a nail from where she had placed them on the cabinet counter and efficiently hung their mutual handiwork.

Emily glanced with pleasure around the fresh white room—at the picture, her plates, the new rug.

"It begins to feel like home."

"Yes," he smiled.

"Well, since that is settled, how about some food?" And Emily proceeded to ladle up hearty bowls of soup.

The dinner went cheerfully. In the general good humor of the occasion even Jason acted civilly enough for them to forget that he was an uninvited guest. As Emily cleared off the plates, Keith settled back in his chair, propped his booted feet up upon an adjoining one, and comfortably lit his pipe.

"Tell me, then, Captain," he spoke to Jason, "what do you trade in with your schooner?"

Jason gave him a quick suspicious look before carefully answering. "Mostly cloth and foodstuffs. We pick up cotton bales from the South, bring them north to the mills, occasionally go down to the Caribbean to pick up molasses and sugar cane."

"Then your business is primarily coastal?"

"Primarily. But from time to time I get the yen for the high seas and more foreign ports, and we put out for Europe."

"What in the world brings you back to a fishing village like East Egg, then?"

Jason's eyes hardened for a moment, but he went on in a light voice. "Even East Egg must have deliveries of the amenities from time to time. After all, the railroad bypassed the town, and the roads in and out are not of the best quality for dray teams."

"Of course. And I suppose someone must transport the salted cod."

"That, too."

"Well, well, I suppose it is an interesting life." Keith puffed contentedly on his pipe.

"It is known to have its moments."

"Yes, I should think so." Keith swung his feet down and prepared to rise. "What do you say, Emily? It is time to check my lamp. Will you join me?"

Emily was wiping the last bowl. "Yes, thank you. And Jason?"

Keith did not give him a chance to answer. "I judge that trudging up the tower stairs would not be the wisest thing for the captain tonight."

"You are probably right. I think I will retire. But first, with your permission, may I inspect some of your books?"

"Help yourself," Keith beamed expansively. And he escorted Emily down the hall to pick up wrappings, then on to the tower corridor, leaving Jason to negotiate his way back to his bed.

"Why the outerwear, Keith?"

"I have set up the telescope on the catwalk, landside. That way, the intermittent flashes of the light toward the sea will not disturb our view of part of the sky."

"Of course. But I did mean to ask you—why does the light flash on and off as it does?"

He smiled at her, then pushed his way through the trap door, pulled himself up and assisted her into the top of the tower. "True, it used to shine continuously, but after some years it was found that on bad nights ships were being confused by all the similar signals. On good clear days, you know, a coastal ship's captain can tell where he is by reading the colors and designs of each lighthouse. Ours, as you know, is white, with the big red cross. Others along the coast are painted equally distinctively, and all different. At night when these designs cannot be seen, most lights appear the same, and a ship could miscalculate its position by twenty or thirty miles, sometimes to its hazard. Now the Lighthouse Service is experimenting with differentiating the light signals themselves. It was a recent directive, and the lampist came and helped me to modify our light to this three-seconds-on-and-three-seconds-off pattern.''

"I know. I timed it."

He looked pleased. "Let's see how observant you are with the stars, my dear." He led her toward the tiny window door that opened onto the catwalk, turned the handle, and let in a blast of frigid air. Then, with a practiced movement, he slid his feet through the opening and in a moment, was outside, reaching a hand in for Emily.

Emily tentatively poked her head through the window, then balked, pulling back to the solid security of the lampbase.

"Are you sure it is quite safe out there for two? The ironwork looks, well, a little shaky."

Keith laughed. "Having second thoughts, my dear? I assure you it is one of the safest spots on the island. The catwalk is critical to the upkeep of the light, and is constantly inspected and repaired."

"But it is so windy. . . ."

"If you'd rather change your mind, I shan't hold it against you. Patience was deathly afraid of heights and never even made it to the top of the tower steps."

That did it. Muttering, "Wither thou goest, I will go," Emily forcefully poked her trousered legs through the opening, realizing it would have been next to impossible, or at least a vastly more dangerous proposition, in skirts. Then she was outside, having her breath torn away from her by a combination of the cold, the wind, and the effect of the relatively unsheltered height. For the catwalk was just a wrought-iron structure around the tower's uppermost circumference. The flooring, if it could be called such, had gaps, inches wide, in its metal grid, and the handrail was just that—a single piece of iron with struts connecting it to the flooring every yard or so. Altogether it was not a situation conducive to peace of mind for one unaccustomed to heights of more than two stories. Emily stood frozen in one position, unsure whether to back up against the rough stone tower wall and window, or to grasp onto the railing for dear life.

Keith watched the various expressions cross her face and laughed. "Come now, my dear, it cannot be as bad as all that! Two steps to your left and you shall be at the telescope."

"Why don't you just bring it two steps toward me, and I won't have to move at all."

He laughed again.

"I do believe you are enjoying my discomfiture, sir."

He muffled his laugh and tried to look contrite in the dim glow of the stars. "I am sorry, but if you could have seen the expression on your face. . . . Well, perhaps it would be best to put off our stargazing for a balmier spring night."

"It is a bit frigid out here."

Without another word, Keith eased her back into the tower, then followed, hauling the telescope with him. Then he turned from shutting the window and took her hands. "Why, you are shaking!"

Emily looked down at her hands which seemed to have a life of their own. "Yes, I suppose I am."

"Well, then, that is certainly enough adventure for this night. It has, at any rate, been a long day. Take yourself off to bed, my dear, and I will join you as soon as duty allows."

Feeling somewhat rebuffed, Emily made her way a bit shamefaced toward the trap door. "I'll try again tomorrow. Perhaps in the daylight. . . ."

"Just a moment, please."

She looked up, and in an instant found his arms engulfing her. "You are not upset with me, then, Keith?"

"My dearest one! I am going to have to change my ways radically. From now on, I shall have to remember to thank God at least once an hour for having brought you into my life."

She snuggled contentedly for a moment as he pressed his lips against her hair, then made her way down to bed.

CHAPTER 8

Feb. 15. After clear day yesterday and early evening, heavy gale of wind sprung up from S to SW about midnight. Damp snow came on early in the morning.

Emily woke and turned from her side to the middle of the bed. With a pang she realized that Keith had never made it down from the tower last night. His pillow was untouched, his sheets cold. Feeling almost bereft, Emily shivered out of her warm coverings into the frigid room and began to prepare for the day. He would be needing to sleep and she had wanted to finally brace herself and go through the rest of Patience's things, so after dressing warmly and peeking out the shutters at the softly falling snow, she lugged Patience's trunk out of the room and across the small hall to the nursery. Leaving it there, she went down to the kitchen to put on a pot of coffee, then wandered up to the tower. There she found Keith stripped of his work shirt, the arms of his woolen underwear shoved up to his elbows, and all the rest of him covered in grease. Squatting amidst bits of machinery, he was looking thoroughly disgruntled.

"What's going on?"

"Oh. Good morning. Is it that late already? The blasted feed line for the oil clogged up on me awhile back and I am trying to sort it out."

He was poking a thin strand of wire through the inch-thick tubing. "There is some kind of an obstruction here, and I can't seem to budge it."

"Does this happen often?"

"On occasion. Usually a bit of blubber that hasn't been properly processed with the oil. Very sloppy of the whalers." He shoved again, and this time succeeded in clearing the tube with a soft pop. He picked up the object to inspect it.

"Whatever is it?"

"Very curious. Seems to be a tiny mouse." He showed her the miniscule oil-drenched object. "Never happened before."

Emily blanched slightly at the greasy creature. "I did not know they existed on the island."

"What's that?" He was already gathering up pieces, preparing to get his lamp in functioning order again. "I'm afraid so. Seem to propagate everywhere. Probably came hiding in the animals' feed at some point."

"So. I guess you'll be wanting some breakfast, and then some sleep after you've put this lot back together."

"That would be nice," he muttered, his mind already back on the equipment.

Giving him one more look, Emily descended again to the kitchen to prepare the food. As she was warming water for Keith to wash up, with, emerged from the study looking hungry.

"Coffee smells good."

"Help yourself."

He did, then made himself comfortable at the table. "How were the stars?"

"What? Oh. It was too cold. Must have been this new storm heading in." She pointed at the thick, softly falling snow outside the window.

"Wet snow. If we are lucky, it will be a harbinger of spring. But then again, it is only mid-February. More likely to be at least several more good blows."

"I certainly hope not," Emily commented worriedly as she pulled a piece of toasted bread away from the coal fire, and impaled another piece onto the prongs of her long iron fork before thrusting it back into the heat below the opened burner.

"This little bit of weather upsets you, does it?" he teased.

"We are so cut off here. It is not like on the mainland where there are neighbors to call upon for help. Think how that last storm just tossed the bell tower into the sea!"

"Yes, it takes some getting used to. On a ship, as well. The smart thing is not to be caught in these northern waters this time of year. I should have been down in the heat near Cuba. But life cannot always be so easily arranged." He paused. "Consider yourself lucky to be snug on this island, such as it is. I've heard tales of ships going down in these waters just from the weight of ice frozen upon their decks and rigging."

"Yesterday morn you sang a different song about the joys of the sailing life."

"One has to use enticement on occasion. And yesterday morning you were in a different mood. Although I can see another change in you today from last evening. More subdued."

"Keith had mechanical problems in the tower."

"That explains much," he commented with a mischievous look.

As if on cue, Keith appeared at the door, looking filthy and exhausted. He muttered a curt "Good morning," then headed for the dry sink with its warm water that he had apparently anticipated. There was silence while he splashed about, then Emily served the meal.

Jason spoke first. "I was thinking of a short stroll outside this morning, to practice my walking."

Keith grunted and swallowed before speaking. "Let it be upon your own head, then. It will be slippery outside."

"I must begin getting up my strength."

Keith eyed him. "If you've so much energy, you might start at the barn to milk the cow and feed the chickens."

"I am afraid my expertise does not extend to the care of livestock."

"I thought not."

Sensing a potential situation, Emily spoke up. "I will take care of the animals. You need your rest, Keith, and Jason would have trouble carrying the milk pail and his walking stick anyway."

Keith gave her a black look. "Thank you, Emily, but I am not as yet totally infirm." And with that he crammed a last bite of toast into his mouth and stomped out of the house.

Jason grinned. "A bit touchy, that one."

Emily kept her silence. She knew her husband to be exhausted, and she herself had not the energy to go through another round with him. After yesterday afternoon she'd expected such behavior to be in the past. With a sigh she rose to tidy up the kitchen, ignoring Jason as he first finished consuming everything edible in sight, then hobbled out the door.

Emily banged a few pots about in general protest to the empty room, then took herself off to the nursery and Patience's trunk.

The small room was freezing. Emily considered lighting the small corner fireplace, then thought better of it and just pulled the woolen shawl more closely about her shoulders. It shouldn't take all that long to go through the lot.

Efficiently she began pulling out the clothing and sorting it into usable and unusable piles. There looked to be the making of another, smaller rug here. She could see that it would have to be in browns and beiges. Quite suitable for the side of the bed on cold mornings. Soon Emily had cleared the trunk down to the underwear level, and could feel the hard bottom of the trunk beneath her fingers. She paused for a moment to judge, looking first inside, then outside the trunk. *Surely there is room for a few more inches of space inside. . . . There must be a false bottom.*

With more of a will, Emily spilled the last of the clothing willynilly on the floor and began prodding the inside edges. Right enough, her fingers felt a small protrusion, and with a snap, she lifted out the false bottom, curious as to what Patience might have been hiding beneath. Pushing the trunk closer to the open dormer window for better light, she surveyed the contents. It did not appear to be much. A small, folded daguerreotype case—Emily lifted the catch to reveal two portraits, a long-bearded Union colonel and a stern-faced woman, staring somberly at each other.

Emily tried to recall the face of Patience the few times she had seen her in church. Yes, these were definitely the parents, and there did not seem to be much love lost between them. Oh, well. She snapped the case shut and reached again into the trunk, this time pulling out a leatherbound book complete with latch. A journal of some kind? As it was unlocked, Emily felt no compunction about opening it at random. It fell open to an entry dated July 27, 1863. Emily scanned the paragraph quickly, then started again at the beginning and read it through slowly.

July 27, 1863—Today Father sent to us a young lieutenant to make his recovery in our house. Father says the conditions in the military hospitals are appalling, and as this Lt. Judson was responsible for saving his life and that of many of his troops at Gettysburg, he feels he owes a debt of honor to him. Mother and I were quite unsure about how to handle this intrusion on our lives, but Father's letter says that Lt. Judson is quite ambulatory, needs only much quiet and consideration to recover from a bad head wound.

Emily paused as she heard footsteps on the stairs. A bit guiltily, she shoved the journal under a pile of clothes. But the footsteps went directly into the bedroom opposite without pausing at her door, and she heard the bed creak as Keith lowered himself into it. Shivering with the cold and possibly the anticipation of the journal, as well, Emily tiptoed down the steps and fetched a pail of coal. In a few minutes the nursery began to warm up with the fire, so she shut the door and retrieved the hidden diary, making herself a seat and pillow of clothes to rest upon before delving in again. Unerringly she opened it to where she'd left off. There was a lapse of a few days between entries.

August 1, 1863—Lt. Judson seems civil enough most of the time. He spends his days sitting on the veranda slowly reading through father's books and dozing. As yet he has not much appetite for such a large man, but Cook is sure that will improve with time. Cook and Maid are both delighted with him and would fuss over him more if he but allowed it. Truth to say, there is something appealing in his tortured eyes.

August 2, 1863—We came back from church this morning to find Lt. Judson in a exceptionally black state of mind. He has been morose before, but the moods seemed to have been short-lived. Afraid he might become violent, and Father so far away on his campaigns, Mother took the precaution of calling in Dr. Gammon. Lt. Judson was not pleased and tried to bodily remove him from the house. The good doctor took it in stride, saying the lieutenant must be suffering from severe headaches at such times. He left morphine for Cook to put in his coffee, and suggested we take the precaution of locking our bedroom doors at night. Mother is all aflutter, and I am not sure what to think.

Emily paused to consider this new bit of information. Keith never had said exactly *how* he'd been wounded. Could he still be feeling ill effects after so many years? And he'd certainly never even intimated that he had been an officer. How had one of his early background and lack of formal education risen to become a lieutenant? With rising curiosity, Emily read on.

August 6, 1863—Lt. Judson was considerably subdued today. Mother sent me to the chemist's shop to purchase an extended supply of morphine. She has left instructions with Cook to lace his coffee each morning with it. He did comment on the bitter flavor at breakfast today, but Cook only smiled and said there was a bit of a coffee shortage and she was extending the household supply with chicory. He accepted the explanation with some grace.

On the way back from the chemist's, I saw a most extraordinary bonnet in the milliner's shop. It was decorated with ostrich plumes, and a long organdy veil. I don't suppose Mother would approve, but if I were to catch Father's ear on his next visit home. . . .

Emily smiled to herself. So Patience had not always been a completely colorless prude. There was still a bit of the coquette in her at this point, even though she must have been over thirty already, and resigned to spinsterhood.

August 8, 1863—Spent the morning with Mother, making bandages with the Ladies' Aid Society. They were all quite curious as to the history of our guest. In accordance with Father's instructions, we said only that he was without family of his own and that we were only doing our Christian duty by him. Still, a few raised eyebrows were evident, and even the obvious age difference between myself and the Lieutenant did not appear to quiet their thoughts. I might add that it is most interesting having a real man about, even one somewhat incapacitated. Since my coming-out some years ago never quite took, I have had little opportunity to be in the company of the opposite gender. Until his arrival, my days were spent with Mother and the household staff, and some occasional church and

135

Aid work. Sometimes, of course, I still wish that Parson Hepwhite had declared himself as we all thought he would five years ago. . . .

Emily grimaced. Patience's portrait of herself was emerging as one uncomfortably close to her own experience. Granted, she herself was a good bit younger than the Patience of 1863, but the necessary concerns were there. Emily had not had the benefit of a house staff or a formal debut, but her upbringing was still fairly solidly middle class within the little community of East Egg. And Emily had had a proposal from a young visiting curate. But he'd been such a pompous little prig that she had never seriously considered the offer, and even her mother had forgiven her this after a few months.

August 10, 1863—Even with the morphine, the Lieutenant's head has been bothering him badly today, so much so that he could not of his own accord follow the words in a book. He asked me if I would read a bit to him, to better pass the time. I had the Bible at hand, but he was working on Julius Caesar's campaigns and asked if I would not mind terribly continuing with them. He was working on the invasion of Britain and I read it at some length. He seemed particularly interested in the landing itself, when Caesar managed to outwit the waiting hordes and disembark further up the coast. As for myself, I weary quickly of all this talk of plunder and laying to waste. Hadn't he enough of it at Gettysburg? And as for Caesar (whom I was first forced to read as a child in the Latin and disliked even then), what profit to learn campaigns from a heathen when the Bible surely has battles enough from which to benefit?

I made bold to venture some of these thoughts but he refused to be taken into conversation, so I continued the readings. He sat on the swing with his eyes closed, and I thought at times perhaps he'd gone to sleep, but as I would pause, he'd open those beautiful eyes and silently beg me to continue.

Good heavens! Was Patience actually falling in love with Keith? Emily knew from her own experience that eventuality was not all difficult, but she hadn't expected it of the prim older woman. Feeling a bit uncomfortable and unwilling to admit the slight twinge of jealousy that had surprised her, Emily shut the journal with a sigh. Perhaps this was not such a good idea, after all. How could she be beginning to feel both sympathy and jealousy for this woman? Almost as an act of penance, she decided to go downstairs and prepare the week's bread for baking.

Emily kneaded dough with a vengeance, her mind still in that faraway time of the summer of 1863. . . . She herself would have been but a slim ten-year-old tomboy waiting excitedly for Father's boat to come in. That was the summer he'd come home from the South, around the Straits of Magellan and up past South America to the cooler waters of the North. He'd been in fine fettle with tales of running the Confederate blockade. She remembered hanging onto him as he unpacked his bag of presents—a lovely large piece of scrimshaw for Mother, and smaller ones for her sisters, etched with flowers and mythical sea creatures.

Emily paused, remembering with delight the horrified look on her mother's face, for Emily's gift of scrimshaw pictured a lovely mermaid sitting in splendor atop a rock, waves lapping at her fish-like tale. She had ecstatically held it in her hands for all of ten seconds before her mother had denounced it as unsuitable for a young lady, snatching it away and relegating it to the all-consuming flames of the kitchen stove. Emily had burst into tears and crawled into her father's lap for comfort, while her little sisters stared, wide-eyed. That was when Father had promised her a special treat, just for the two of them, and had organized the boat trip out past the lighthouse. . . .

Emily was still smiling to herself at the memory when she was distracted by the slamming of the outside door. She listened to the now distinctive three-legged shuffle coming down the hall and, a moment later, welcomed Jason into the kitchen with a smile. His thick head of hair and beard were damp, with a few soft flakes of snow still sticking to them, and the unbearded bits of his cheeks had taken on a considerably healthier-looking, ruddy glow.

"Had a good walk?"

He smiled back. "I do believe I hobbled over every inch of your domain." He settled into a chair by the table, then rubbed his hands for warmth. "There would not be a chance of some hot coffee, would there?"

"Positively. You'll find that the coffeepot is practically always warming on the stove. If no one is about, just help yourself."

"Thank you, and I shall."

Emily served him, covered her dough for rising, then helped herself to a cup and sat down as well.

"Did you take part in the War Between the States?"

"What?" He looked surprised.

"A simple question, certainly."

"Well, no. That is, not directly. I was at sea most of

the time. Busy working my way up on an Atlantic trader. Why do you ask?''

''Keith was wounded in the fighting. I was merely looking for another opinion on the event.''

''Well, it certainly did eliminate certain very lucrative sea routes.''

''What are you referring to?''

''The slavers, of course.''

''Surely you were not a party to that!''

''Are you always such an innocent, Emily? It was not only whales and cotton mills which brought prosperity to New England. In a much larger sense, it was slaves.''

''But the abolition movement was always strongest in New England.''

''Of course the great shipping magnates of Boston and Providence opposed slavery in their own domains. They had no great plantations that needed cheap labor. But condemning the practice in public did not keep them from building their fortunes on the trade privately.''

''So you've been to Africa?''

''Not as my own master, but yes, I've been there.''

''You had no compunctions about the job?''

''I'll say this—I've been on cleaner-smelling ships.''

Emily groaned. ''You really are quite heartless.''

''Not at all. Someone must do the dirty work, and it paid well. A ship's officer usually receives a percentage of a successful cargo.''

''Just as with the whales?''

''Just so.''

Emily rose to check her dough and stoke the fire in the stove. So her husband had been wounded while

139

fighting a cause which this man had helped to flourish. She was only now beginning to understand part of the instant antipathy between the two. It was not only a question of their somewhat mutual interest in herself. In his own way Keith had instantly recognized a basic philosophical difference between himself and Jason. Captain Cobb was really more than a little bit of a pirate.

She turned to face him again, her face flushed by a combination of her recent proximity to the coals and her thoughts.

"When do you expect your men to brave the weather and come for you?"

"Aha! You begin to relish the absence of your prize boarder!"

"Not at all . . . It's just that. . . ."

"It is just that I am perhaps a bit too wild for your cloistered existence here. It is, after all, the perfect place to avoid the rest of the world."

"You know that is not true. Besides, people usually take their troubles with them—even to barren islands."

"Remarkably astute. You learn quickly."

"I have no choice. Now, unless you wish to assist me in scrubbing the kitchen floor, I would suggest you go and have a rest before lunch."

"What a wonderful thing is woman. When she is backed up against the wall, she is capable of clearing the decks merely by expressing the necessity of scrubbing them. And this particular deck, I might add, already appears to be remarkably clean."

"If the captain does not wish a well-aimed pot to connect with his head, he will make a quick exit."

"Your point is well made, madam." With a grin Jason escaped to his private den.

Emily sighed. What *had* made her suggest scrubbing the floor? Now she'd just have to carry out her threat. After another sigh, she collected bucket, water, and scrub brush and got on her knees to begin the detested chore. And why had she chased him out of her kitchen domain? Probably fear of the same combination of ruthlessness and charm to which she'd been attracted from the beginning. Shifting her thoughts with an effort, Emily meditated for a while upon Patience. How often had Keith's first wife performed this same onerous task, and with what enthusiasm? Surely, it must have come even harder for her, with her former reliance on servants. With some chagrin, Emily felt herself being drawn back to the journal waiting in the nursery. Maybe she'd allow herself just one little peek after lunch. . .

As she rose from her knees to put the bread in the oven, Emily glanced out the window. The soft snow was still falling. There would be no respite from the weather for a while yet. Maybe something special for lunch would improve everyone's spirits. She racked her brains for a few minutes, then decided to make some fresh broad noodles, a major task in itself. With them she could prepare a casserole with the last bits of bacon, and the soft curd cheese that seemed to be the best she could do with Flora's excess milk.

And maybe a pudding for desert. She wished she'd requested some flavorings, or at least some tapioca from the mainland. Well, she'd just have to use her imagination. Maybe some port would do in lieu of vanilla. . . .

An hour and a half of concerted labor, and many

good smells later, Keith appeared in the kitchen looking considerably improved.

"What are you doing up already?"

He actually smiled. "Certain aromas have been drifting up the stairs. They would not allow me to lie about a minute longer."

"Let us hope the aromas and your stomach are correct. I fear that lunch is much in the way of an experiment."

"It must be a grand one. It smells like Christmas."

"Save the compliments until after you've tasted it, please." But she couldn't help smiling. "You seem much improved. Is your head feeling better, then?" Not until she saw the look on his face did she realize her mistake.

His eyes clouded over with suspicion. "How did you know about my head?"

Emily thought quickly. "Relax, husband. I was only putting two and two together. You had mentioned a war wound, and the rest of your body appears quite fit. But you do seem in pain on occasion."

He scowled.

"Why don't you tell me about it, and then if I know the old pain is coming on, I can have more patience, er . . . that is, more forbearance with you."

Still scowling, he sat down.

"And what, pray tell, is so terrible about being concerned about my husband's welfare?"

"Enough, woman. All right. It was a scattering of grapeshot I caught at Gettysburg through sheer stupidity."

"Surely being wounded in a battle is more a matter of chance than stupidity."

142

"It was stupidity. I myself had forced my men to dig and secrete themselves in a trench so they would have less chance of having their heads blown off, and also less temptation to retreat while the battle raged about us. I was devising a bit of a mirror for a periscope to peek over the top. Unsatisfied with the results, I poked my head up and caught the grapeshot. The surgeons subsequently removed most of it, but a piece or two were too heavily embedded for safe removal, so they left it there. Even so, many years later I sometimes feel addled by it."

Emily wiped her hands and went to stand behind his chair. Gently she began to massage his temples, moving her fingers slowly backward in the thick hair, till she felt several hard spots on his scalp. He jumped.

"Does that hurt?"

"No. Only the discomfort of sharing it with some-one else."

"And what do you think I am here for, then? Should we not be sharing everything with each other?"

He sighed and gradually reached his hands back to catch hers, and pull them around his shoulders. Slowly he kissed first her fingers, then the palms of her hands. Then he maneuvered her around, into his lap. She cuddled silently, satisfied for the moment.

"Aha! Made up again, have we?"

Emily and Keith both jumped at Jason's words, Emily right out of Keith's arms.

"And where is your third leg, sir?" roared Keith.

"Resting in my room. My little jaunt outside this morning gave me considerably more confidence, would you not say?"

"I would say you had confidence enough already, and a damnable nerve, too, sneaking up on people like that."

"Nothing personal intended, my dear chap." And with a wicked grin Jason slid into his chair, then blithely asked, "What is for lunch?"

Fuming silently, Emily practically threw her casserole onto the table.

"My, aren't we techy," chided Jason, as he helped himself to a heaping plateful of the savory concoction.

Able to withstand it no longer, Emily blurted out, "Captain Cobb, if you cannot keep a more civil tongue in your head, I shall have to ask you to take this and all further meals in your own room."

Jason raised his glass of milk to his hosts. "I'm sick of this island, and I'm sick of milk! A grown man drinks rum, not milk! I'm beginning to grow stir-crazy in your idyllic abode. But, pardon me, I shall try to comply with your rigid standards of social etiquette in the future."

Emily and Keith stared, then continued the rest of the meal in silence. After both men had drifted out of the kitchen in separate directions, Emily put the dirty dishes and utensils in order, then decided on a breath of air for herself, too, before facing the rest of the day. Rather than venture out into the soft wetness, she climbed the stairs of the tower. Once on top, she was struck again by the world of stark beauty which surrounded her. On impulse, she opened the window to the catwalk and allowed the cold air to envelop her senses. After inhaling deeply, she was preparing to close off the outside world once more when she heard footsteps behind her.

"Pray do not let me interfere with your mystical experience."

Emily whirled about. "Jason! What are you doing here?"

"Just some further explorations." And with that he grabbed her roughly about the waist and shoulder and forced his lips on hers.

Emily could not believe what was happening. She knew she had done nothing to encourage such liberties. Filled with rage, she struggled mightily, summoned up one last reserve of strength, and swiftly brought up her knee into his groin. He staggered against her for a moment, fighting the pain, then allowed her to maneuver his body to the still open window. There, she shoved his head outside and with a quick motion slid the window partially closed against his head and shoulders, imprisoning him for the moment.

"You need a bit of cooling off, Captain." She spoke in a voice trembling with delayed shock.

His response was an oath.

On shaking legs, Emily let herself through the trap door and down the stairs. She headed straight for the nursery where she took the precaution of shutting and barricading the door with Patience's trunk before reigniting the fire, then settled down with a moan to try to calm her racing heartbeat. Pray God, Jason's men would come for him very soon. She could not stand much more of this seesawing tension between herself and the two men. And where had Keith been all this time? She gasped with the thought of what could still occur if he had been outside and had spied the two silhouettes in the tower. . . .

Ever so slowly Emily felt her blood pressure

returning to normal. After a few more minutes she stirred, reached for the hidden journal, and let if fall open on her lap once more.

September 5, 1863—We received a telegram from Father today. He is being given a brief leave and will be home tomorrow! The household is in an uproar. Cook is busily preparing his favorite foods and Mother and I have been working like dervishes all day helping Maid to complete the housecleaning. I dusted father's library and arranged flowers all over the house. Maid requested my assistance in pounding the carpets, but really one cannot expect a woman in my position to cover herself with dust!

Even the Lieutenant has been contributing. He insisted he was well enough to trim and tidy the yard rather than have Mother hire one of the local men. I must say, he does begin to look more fit, although his eyes have recently taken on a glazed and wooly look. . . .

Emily paused, perplexed. Keith's eyes seemed to have been the focus of Patience's attentions all along. And now there was something odd about them. She pondered anew, until a few lines of verse popped into her head.

For he on honeydew hath fed.
And drunk the milk of Paradise.

Where, oh where, had she seen them? She pulled herself to her feet and was heading to the volume of poetry in her own trunk when it came to her, and she returned to her cushioned seat with a sigh. Of course. It was Coleridge. *Kubla Khan.* Coleridge had been a notorious opium-eater. And was not morphine derived from opium? They've gone and gotten Keith addicted to morphine! Those poor benighted women! And what of Keith, becoming more and more distracted, and unaware of the source? Rabidly Emily picked up the book again.

September 7, 1863—Father's homecoming was indeed an occasion. We supped royally last night, during which Father regaled us with tales of the campaign. He says there are now women assisting in the hospitals and sometimes on the fields themselves. I pointed out that it was all well and good for the women to support their men by making bandages and such, but surely the battlefield was no place for a woman of birth. He gave me a look then that I did not understand and merely said that some women of birth did not feel that way, and men whose lives had been saved did not either. But really, it is most lower-class. I should feel like a camp follower!

After the dessert Father took the Lieutenant to his study for a little talk. Wonder of wonders! It transpires that the Lieutenant and I shall wed! Father gently asked me if I were willing, of course. He says that Keith is quite mellow now and will make a fine addition to the family and community. He spoke briefly of the Lieutenant's past, saying that Judson (as my father calls him) brought himself up "by his own bootstraps" and was intelligent, but self-educated. Father felt that the proof of the pudding was surely to be seen in the Lieutenant's demeanor during the stress of battle. He was brave and a born leader in these situations, as seen by his rise from private to officer by dint of daring and courage. His men fearlessly followed him into the fray. Surely I would be willing to take a chance on such a man, particularly at my time in life. I fear I was much taken by the romance of my father's words and accepted the offer quite willingly. Father wants to be here for the event, so a private ceremony has been set for the forthcoming Sunday, before Father must return to the war. How will Mother and I ever prepare the gown in time?

Emily stifled a small smile. Keith did seem to have a proclivity for instant marriages.

September 12, 1863—The wedding is tomorrow. The gown is actually completed—white silk, with ribbon trimmings, and because the weather is turning cool now, an over mantle as well, trimmed with lace and braid. Mother even purchased new crinolines and a morning cap of lace. She asked Father if the expense of it all were too great and he exploded, rather uncharacteristically in her presence, "Hang the expense! I'll have my girl a beauty for her day!" Keith should look handsome, too. Maid has been polishing the brass on his dress uniform.

Father and Mother both took me aside separately to discuss what they called "the marriage duty." I must say that they cast little light on the subject, aside from leaving me even more curious. Father has even hired a horse and buggy to take us the few miles to the hotel at the sea for a week of "honeymoon." After that, we are to stay with Mother until such time as we deem a house of our own suitable.

Will tomorrow never come?

Emily felt a stab of envy. Patience had received the trimmings she'd been denied in her own recent wedding—expectation, gown, and private holiday with her new husband. They did, however, have two things in common, the groom and the sea. Nothing could have pulled Emily away from Patience's journal now.

September 14, 1863—It is raining. Still, my husband has gone out for some sea air after lunch. His head seems to be bothering him again. We passed a silent morning in the hotel room, walking around each other, unsure what to say after last night. It certainly was not what I had

148

expected. Surely women are doubly cursed. But if Mother has managed to put up with it all these years. . .

Emily grinned. It had taken some time, but it would appear that she was definitely one up on Patience. She would willingly forget about all the missing ingredients of a formal wedding for yesterday's hour of bliss. She paused to remember the marvelous sense of oneness, of being cherished and held. There had to be more moments like that. And she knew Keith had felt the same . . . She would allow herself one more entry into the saga of Patience, then close the book forever.

September 18, 1863—I am at my wits' end. My husband has not been himself all week, and his condition is worsening. That he has been in obvious pain, I can forgive, but his ranting and raving is increasing in intensity. Today he frightened the other lodgers at breakfast by overturning first the coffeepot, and then the entire breakfast table. That done, he stormed out to the sea, and I followed for only a moment. Only a moment, because I could hear him howling at the waves, all the while grabbing his head as if to wrest if off his body. Whatever is to be done?

The coffeepot. Yes! The coffeepot was the key. Patience must have forgotten to bring the daily dose of morphine, and neither he nor Patience was aware of the effect! What would happen next?

September 20, 1863—We arrived home exhausted and distraught. Thank God, Father was not here to see us. I cried in Mother's arms and she said that I would learn to bear up under the strain. To try to put it out of my mind. I had not the heart to tell her the rest—his days of screaming in the wind.

149

And then this morning. He came to breakfast early and caught Cook slipping the usual paper of powders into his coffee. He looked at her unbelievingly, forced her to present the supply of morphine. He tasted a few grains with his fingertip, then spat them out. Soon Cook was in tears, confessing the length of time he'd been administered the drug. I think she feared he would strangle her, so fierce was his look, but he only whirled around the room and walked out, pausing at the door to say that when we'd all tired of poisoning him and desired his presence once more, he could be found at the sea.

Emily closed the journal with a snap. This information was too volatile for her to continue reading in any kind of conscience. But it explained so much. Particularly Keith's constant reservation about getting too close to another human being. He had been hurt badly, even if unintentionally. However had he managed to return to Patience and another ten years of marriage?

Emily looked speculatively at the journal. The answers were probably there, but had she any right to pursue them? Would it not be better to proceed as they were, a measure or two more of confidence each day until he could wholeheartedly put his trust in her? Feeling extremely torn, but also virtuous, Emily got to her feet, picked up the journal, and prepared to cast it into the flames of the fireplace.

Then, instead, she placed it in its hiding place beneath the false bottom of Patience's trunk.

Emily walked to the dormer window. The weather was turning colder again. The damp snow of earlier in the day had now changed to small hard pellets, whirled by the wind in the failing light. For a passing moment she wondered what it was like in the sun, in uncomplicated places like Africa, or around southern isles with palm trees swaying. Her father had described them, even given her a scrimshaw brooch with a palm tree etched into it . . . and Jason had tried to tempt her briefly with a vision of such warm climes. She knew it would never be hers to see. Her destiny was here, on this desolate isle.

Shivering, Emily let herself out the door and downstairs to the hall where she donned her warm outerwear. It was time to seek Keith.

She found him, head lowered onto his arms atop his workbench in the barn. She walked up to him slowly, placed her own arms gently around his shoulder.

He raised his head. "Leave me alone."

"Keith, Keith! What is the matter?" she whispered.

Halfheartedly he tried to disengage himself without turning to look at her. "Look into your own heart and conscience for the answer, woman."

"Please. I have nothing to hide. What is it?"

He turned finally, and she saw the pain in his eyes, not a physical pain this time, but a look of betrayal. "This afternoon, after lunch . . ."

She finished for him. "You glanced up at the tower."

"Yes." That one word was full of defeat.

"You saw two figures."

"Yes."

"Then you looked away and stomped off to the barn."

"Yes."

"Your lack of faith in me is all too obvious. Could

151

you not have watched for another minute to learn what really resulted from that embrace?"

Keith refused to meet her eyes.

"Then, again, you could have raced up the tower to rescue me."

"It did not appear you desired rescuing."

"But you did not even stop to find out, did you? You just tramped off to your personal sanctuary to lick your wounds." Emily was annoyed. "What kind of a man are you, anyway? Even a cuckold, which you are not, has enough pride left to avenge himself." She was shouting now. "Were I a man, things would go differently!"

Keith continued to sit there, spiritless. Emily gazed at him a few moments more, then walked out in disgust. When she returned to the house, Jason's door was also tightly closed.

Fine, she thought to herself. Let them both stew in their own juices for a while. She viciously attacked a new loaf of bread with a knife, almost slicing several fingers in the process. And why should she cook for them? She slathered butter on two slices, poured a glass of milk for herself, and balancing carefully, managed to negotiate the food and a lantern up the stairs to the nursery. They both had their places of retreat. Well, then, let this be hers. After refueling the fireplace, she stood by the window, watching snow drift through the early darkness.

He'd be coming to start up his light now. Another night with Keith in the tower; herself, in an empty bed. It was becoming absurd. Every obstacle she surmounted with Keith seemed to lead to another. If only Jason had not chosen their wedding night to shipwreck himself . . . Or if he'd chosen another island on which to be cast. No. Even now, she could not wish drowning upon him.

In a moment of despondency, Emily cast her eyes out into the night again. *Lord, you made this freezing beauty, and one day it will melt into spring. . . . Can you not also help me to thaw the ice in my husband's heart?''*

The answer was so obvious. The captain must leave their island. Let him prey upon some other innocent—or not so innocent—one. There must be a multitude of women ready to relinquish their all for a man like Jason. She was not about to become one of them. At least Keith was not a womanizer. If she could only get him on an even keel again, he would be rock steady, and wear solidly and well through the years. *Poor Keith*. That was probably Patience's initial estimation of him as well. . . . *Patience and Keith*. Did she really want to continue resurrecting the ghost of their relationship? Again, Emily was drawn to the trunk and the journal. . . .

November 1, 1863—My husband returned home today. His period of absence has been a most difficult time for Mother and myself. There had to be a story to give out to curious friends and neighbors. We said he'd been called back to the war as an adjutant to my father, praying no one would learn the truth. Still, the smell of scandal hung over us. I sought consolation in the Lord, almost praying he would never return. . . .

He is healthy, bronzed, and with new muscles. He says he found work as a fisherman. Imagine! If the Ladies' Aid Society would hear of that! Why did he return? Nothing would have forced me to go after him. . . .

Emily found her hackles raised. Over a month and a half since Keith's disappearance, and they had not searched for him! She was suddenly beginning to dislike Patience intensely. What a self-centered little prima donna! And why *had* Keith returned? Emily knew the answer before asking it of herself. *Duty.* Keith took his vows seriously. He had taken the time to get himself well, now understanding the cause of at least part of his illness. That done, he had returned to his commitments.

November 2, 1863—Mother gave him another bedroom last night. He did not protest. Neither did he attempt to visit me. (I had, at any rate, bolted my door.) Today he went to visit Mr. Goodkin in his dry goods store, and finalized negotiations Father had begun for him before our wedding. As Mr. Goodkin has no heir, my husband will be buying a half share in the business—with Father's money, I should add. He has none of his own. At least the business should keep him out of the house the better part of most days.

I have been feeling peaked lately, and my stomach is not happy with Cook's rich meals. It must be the general stress of the times.

Emily paused at the last two sentences. Was it possible . . . ? She quickly flipped a few pages further along in the journal.

December 5, 1863—I feared the worst, and now it is certain. I am pregnant with his child. My days have been hell with the thought and pain of it. No! It is inconceivable that I should accept the results of one night's lying with him as a lifetime burden. Mother agrees. She says she has heard of an old African woman who knows how to fix these things.

154

Emily gasped. This woman was about to kill Keith's baby! The baby he had so desired!

December 10, 1863—It is done. He shall never know. And he shall never have the opportunity to do it to me again.

Incredible. How could anyone do such a vile thing? And Keith never knowing, always blaming his own inadequacy, or Patience's health on his lack of family. Did she feel no remorse, or was that to come later with her reversion into herself and her misinterpretations of the Bible, as if she could find forgiveness for her own murderous deed?

December 25, 1863—He has been most considerate of my extended weakness these past days, neither knowing nor guessing the cause. He presented me with a lovely bonnet I'd been desiring from the milliner's as a Christmas present. The rest of the festivities were subdued, with Father still at war and casualty lists mounting. I made my husband a bit of needlework for his bedroom wall, from Scripture. . . .

The hypocrite! Emily was becoming mightily fed up. She rose, stretched, paced the confines of the tiny room a few times before finding the food she'd left on the window sill and absentmindedly consuming it. If that detestable woman were still alive, she would have quite happily throttled her. But it was silly to work herself up like this. Patience and her journal were very much in the past. Unfortunately, the results were still preying upon Keith, and he was now Emily's own husband. Something had to be done. But what? She paced around a few more times, thinking. Well, why not try the obvious? Instead of ignoring him and his foul frame of mind for another long night, why not try

155

to reverse it by distracting him from his misery? It was a ploy that Patience had certainly never used.

Determined at last, Emily marched across the hall and into their bedroom. She rummaged in her trunk until she found an unusual item of her trousseau, a frilly summer nightgown. Swiftly donning it, she then stood shivering in the too scant bit of cotton and lace and examined herself by the dim glow of the lantern in the mirror over the dresser.

Her hair. Yes. It would have to be undone and brushed. She pulled out pins, then administered long brush strokes well past the count of one hundred. She gave herself another good look. Something else was needed. She returned to the trunk and pulled out a little japanned box of red and black lacquer. Inside lay her personal crown jewels, a lifetime of presents from Father. She removed a scrimshaw brooch decorated with a palm tree waving in tropical breezes, gentle waves lapping close to the sand at its trunk. Mounting it on her one golden chain, she carefully hung it around her neck, then observed the result. Excellent. But something was missing.

An alluring scent. Again she went to the trunk and found another of Father's gifts, a bottle of perfume she'd never used. She opened it, gave it a tentative sniff, then dashed it liberally behind ears, on wrists, neck, and breast. Emily smiled. Maybe she'd over-done it just a bit. She did reek of something akin to sandalwood, coconut, and orchids. Oh well, no retreating now. She started for the door, gird for battle, then returned for her shawl and woolen socks to cover her feet. She could always abandon them at the tower trap door.

Emily picked up the lantern and carefully tiptoed

down the stairs to the tower corridor. The study door was open, and there was light emanating from the kitchen. She took a deep breath and rushed past both doorways, hoping she'd remain unseen by the captain. Then she ran as fast as her flimsy skirt would allow her to the tower steps, and up.

She was puffing and disheveled by the time she reached the trap door. Not the calm, seductive image she'd wished to present, certainly. Emily balanced there for a minute, trying to calm herself, to rearrange her carefully orchestrated appearance and frame of mind. But before she was able to push open the door and emerge, as in a vision, it was opened for her. She looked up into Keith's face, peering down.

"What is going on here? It sounded like an invasion of elephants."

"It is only myself."

"Well, come up, then," he said, and he reached down a hand for assistance.

Emily struggled through, trying to retain some measure of dignity.

He looked at her. "What are you trying to do dressed like that, give me another case of pneumonia to nurse? And whatever is that ghastly smell?"

Emily looked at him, sniffed twice, then burst into tears.

"It is an exotic perfume, and my best summer nightgown, and I was only hoping to comfort you. And you've gone and ruined everything!" She sank onto the floor in a pathetic bundle, and tried to wipe her eyes with the corners of her shawl.

Keith looked at her in disbelief, then burst out laughing. He continued roaring as if he were unable to stop, each new peal setting Emily off into a fresh paroxysm of sobbing. Then he was down on his knees, trying to gather her up in his arms.

"I will say this for you, Emily"—a pause to wipe his own tearing eyes—"you do keep a man guessing. I have great difficulty in staying angry with you for any length of time, deserving or not."

She sniffled again. "Am I forgiven, then?"

"For what?"

"For whatever it is you think I did that I shouldn't have, and certainly did not do in any event."

He hugged her to him. "I would probably forgive you anything—with one exception."

She looked really worried. "What is that?"

"The wretched scent you have spilled upon yourself. It is near impossible to remain within breathing distance. Would you kindly go and scrub it off!"

Emily burst into tears again, this time only half real. "I cannot!"

"And why, pray tell?"

"The water is in the kitchen, and so is the captain."

Keith's face turned grim. "That villain has been bothering you again! It is high time I did something about it!"

"No! No, please. Just do not allow me the opportunity to be alone with him. He cannot control his own nature any more than you can control your moods."

"But he does not have grapeshot in his skull."

"True. But leave him be. His boat cannot be long in coming now. I cannot face further dissension."

"All right, then. I will escort you to the bedroom, and fetch the water myself. But I shall have to return here. The oil lines are still malfunctioning slightly, and they need constant attention. When his boat comes I will at least be able to send with it a letter to the

Lighthouse Service authorities requesting immediate assistance to replace the fog bell and these lines." He extricated himself and rose. "Come."

She followed, and within half an hour had been scrubbed, kissed chastely on the cheek, and tucked into bed like a small child. He paused at the door and grinned at her mischievously before leaving her with a parting shot: "How much better is thy love than wine! and the smell of thy ointments than all spices!"

CHAPTER 9

*Feb. 16. Snow turned to hail with small gale winds from
N to NE late afternoon and evening. This morning clear
and cold at 15°. Oil lines still sluggish, but seem to
contain no further impediments.*

Emily rose early and decided it was time to cast
from her mind the journal and other nonsense of the
previous day and get down to some practical work.
She spread her woolen cloth on the kitchen table and
began to measure and cut. By the time Keith appeared
from the tower to milk Flora, she had begun to baste
together her new pair of trousers. And on his return,
pail in hand, she forced him to model for her the
pieces of his new shirt so she could pin it for a suitable
fit. And this before his first cup of coffee. He
grumbled mildly, but succumbed to her puttering,
apparently pleased by her constructive mood.

Emily removed a final pin from her mouth, then
stood back to observe the result on her husband.

"The shirt will work handsomely, I think. How did your night go? Were you able to get any sleep?" Chalk marks made, she began to remove the cloth from his back and arms.

"A few cat naps, Emily. I am not as exhausted as yesterday, but feel a good ten hours sleep would do no harm."

"Then you shall have it. Directly after breakfast."

"I do not intend to leave you alone all day with our guest."

"Fear not. If he comes within five paces, I shall aim a few pins at him."

Keith laughed. "Seriously, my dear, we will have to come up with a better defense than that."

She thought a moment. "If a bit of light will not disturb you, you may carry the rocking chair upstairs, and I shall sew while you sleep. There is more than enough to keep me busy."

He laughed again. "In my profession, a 'bit of light' is never a deterrent to sleep. I've had to spend too many nights in the tower. It sounds like an excellent solution."

"Fine. Let us have some breakfast, then."

Emily had just served up their porridge when Jason appeared from his lair. He was using his crutch. Keith gave him a cool, but polite "Good morning," and asked if his legs were troubling him.

"I seem to have overexerted myself on all fronts yesterday," muttered Jason ruefully with a glance at Emily. He sank into his chair with an almost audible creak of muscles, then began spooning up the bowl of breakfast Emily had placed in front of him.

They ate in silence, none of them willing to take the chance of rehashing the events of the day before.

161

Finally sated, Keith rose and began to remove the rocking chair.

Jason watched questioningly, then asked, "Are you planning some housecleaning?"

"Nothing like that. Emily desired the chair upstairs for a while."

"Oh." As if that explained everything. "And what am I supposed to do with myself for another long day?"

"You might rest, or even meditate upon your past life," smiled Emily sweetly. "I would be happy to fetch the Bible for you, sir."

"It's come to that, has it! Well, then, to clear the air, let it be known that I will be just as pleased to leave this frigid sanctuary as the two of you will be to have me go!" And with a snort he collected his stick and shuffled back to the study, slamming the door behind him.

Keith gave Emily a smile. "Shall we ascend to our boudoir, my dear?"

"Why not?"

Apparently Keith was really tired, for he was asleep almost before his boots were removed. Emily gave him a rueful glance as she tucked the quilt over him. So much for her secret hopes of a beautiful reconciliation that morning. She sat in the rocker next to the window's light and began to stitch, mulling all the while over the vast swings in her husband's temperament. After yesterday afternoon's dejection, his laughter and tenderness of the night had been a shock. Even she had not expected such a result from her "seduction" attempt. Perhaps Father's exotic perfume had done its job after all. Still, it might not be a bad idea to pour out the rest of it at the first opportunity. Then again, it could be preserved indefinitely as a secret weapon. . . . Emily smiled at the direction her thoughts were taking . . . *Now, Lord, please. It is time. Let Jason's boat arrive!*

As if in answer to her prayer, Emily heard a sudden tapping on the stairs. She rose in some confusion, scattering her sewing on the floor around her feet. In a thrice she was at the door, then peering down the steps. Jason was standing there, preparing to bang at the banister again with his stick.

"Whatever is it, Jason?"

"My boat! My boat is coming!"

"Are you sure?"

"I stepped out for a breath of air. The sky and sea are clear. It is unmistakably the longboat from the *Juliana.*"

"I'll go and wake Keith."

"No. Let him rest a little longer. It will be some time before they arrive. I will walk down and help them pull the boat in."

Emily was halfway down the steps. "I can help, as well."

"You'd best remain here. Perhaps you'd not mind preparing something to warm them. . . ."

"Of course. They enjoyed my chowder last time. Perhaps another pot . . ."

"Excellent!" And Jason hobbled with spirit out of the cottage, excitement in his eyes.

Emily happily set a big pot on the stove and began to throw ingredients into it. *At last Keith and I shall have our chance at privacy and happiness,* she thought. Yes, there would still remain a few ghosts to bury, but she was convinced that it could be done. She began to hum to herself as she worked, and when the cottage door burst open a half-hour later, she bustled cheerfully into the hall to welcome her deliverers.

They came in what looked like a caravan. First Jason, empty-handed save for his stick, then the three men she remembered so well, and whose picture hung on her wall. The sailors were loaded down with boxes which they deposited in a row in her kitchen. Emily hadn't even time to greet them before they were out the door again. Jason stayed, shrugging off his coat and heaving himself into a chair.

"What is all this?" asked Emily in wonderment, staring at the boxes. "It looks like Christmas!"

"I understand it is the ransom payment for my handsome self," joked Jason.

"Well, I'll admit that I did accede to their suggestion that they bring a few supplies, but. . . ." She looked at the boxes in awe.

"Go ahead, open them. More is on the way. The boat appeared loaded to the gunwales."

"I will have to wake Keith first. He mustn't miss this." And before Jason could protest, Emily was on her way to the bedroom.

Keith groaned, but arose quickly enough when Emily explained the excitement. Not taking the time to pull on his boots, he carried them downstairs where he sank into a chair opposite Jason. Still somewhat in a daze, he watched Emily begin to explore the cases. The first she opened was filled exclusively with hanks of brightly colored woolen yarns.

"Did they buy out the entire mercantile store?" she asked in amazement as she pulled out hank after hank of the yarn. "I shall be able to knit sweaters and socks enough for an army with this."

Jason looked pleased. "My men do not stint when it comes to the important things."

The next box was filled with tins of teas and spices. Many of them Emily had only read about. She pulled out samples, reading the exotic labels: "Paprika . . . cinnamon . . . Darjeeling tea . . . dill . . . black pepper . . . ginger root . . . basil . . . oregano . . . Earl Grey tea . . . tarragon . . . thyme . . . and more. What fun we shall have with all of these!"

Then she moved to the third box, and had just let out a whoop of delight when the three men reappeared with another load. Emily looked up at them. "You have outdone yourselves, gentlemen. Surely this box of books was not found in East Egg?"

Pert, the first mate, looked a bit uncomfortable with the praise. "Well, now, Red wanted to visit an old auntie in Portsmouth anyhow"—here he paused to wink broadly at the captain—"and he wasn't sure exactly what to choose, so he just told the bookshop people to pack up a box full of something nice."

Something nice seemed to consist of entire matching sets of Dickens and Sir Walter Scott, as well as three volumes by Melville, the most recent edition of *Godey's Lady's Book*, two cookbooks, a volume of Celia Thaxter's poetry, and a magnificent edition of Matthew Brady's photographs of the Civil War. Not to mention recent copies of *Harper's Weekly* and other periodicals.

Keith spoke up then. "We cannot accept all of this. There is no way I could ever pay you back on my salary . . ."

"Nonsense," Jason answered as he grandly waved his cohorts off again. "What am I to do with yarn and books on my ship? Most of the men cannot even read;

165

and they certainly do not knit." He seemed highly pleased by Keith's discomfiture. "Do continue, Emily. This is vastly entertaining."

Emily moved to the three hogsheads that had just been deposited on her kitchen floor. Sugar, hard biscuit crackers, and a barrel filled to the brim with pickles! She pried open the latter, and presented samples to the men. Keith chomped on one meditatively, then picked up his boots and made for the door.

"Where are you going, Keith?"

"Back to bed. You may wake me when this madness is over and done with." And with a final growl he stamped off.

"Your husband does not seem very adept at gift-taking."

Emily stared after him. "No. He's not had much practice, I think." She shook her head at his bad grace, then collapsed into a chair with a pickle of her own.

The men came back three times more, and Emily sat in a daze watching the growing piles of smoked hams, sides of bacon, smoked turkey, geese, and fish, as well as further barrels of grains and cereals, potatoes, and assorted dried fruits.

"It really is too much, too much," she said at last.

Jason had been watching her face silently the while. "You have chosen not to believe me prior to this, but I really can afford it."

"How?" Emily had never seen such largess in one pile.

"Yours not to ask, Emily."

"It is the cave, is it not?"

166

He looked more than startled, and she realized her error too late.

"What about the cave, Emily?" A new hardness had crept into his voice.

"Nothing at all, Jason," she tried to cover herself quickly. "Just a few words you muttered while feverish."

He pounded the table in anger. "Out with it, woman!"

Emily just looked at this new side of Jason in some awe. Luckily her answer was saved by the final return of the men. They innocently unloaded their last burdens, then gathered around the table for a well-deserved lunch.

"Left the fodder and grain for the animals in the barn," Pert broke the silence as he was served.

Emily tried to smile brightly for him. "I do not know how to thank you for this bounty, Mr. Pert. You've quite outdone yourself. I had expected a few pounds of this and that. . . ."

"My pleasure, missus. Gave us somewhat to do while waiting for the weather to clear." Then he quickly turned his attention to the chowder.

Emily sat watching the men wolf down their meal. All but Jason. He was absent-mindedly tap, tap, tapping his stick on the kitchen floor, glowering all the while. Finally, the sailors could eat no more, and they rose to head for the door.

"Thankee once more, Missus Judson," as Pert tipped his hat. "I'll say it again. You *do* make a fine chowder." the other men nodded their assents and Emily gave them a lovely smile.

"Anytime you're near Hazard Island, you are welcome to stop in for more."

"Aye. We might at that," grinned Pert, showing a mouth with entirely too few teeth. "And now, Cap'n, we'd best be off while the elements are with us."

"Don't you think I know the sea's temper as well as you!" thundered Jason.

"No offense meant, Cap'n. Just makin' conversation, so to speak," and with a quick look at the sudden storm in his captain's eyes, Pert scurried out, quickly followed by the other two.

"You've no cause to rebuke your men like that, Jason," Emily admonished mildly. "Especially when they think the sun and moon set upon you."

Ignoring her remark, Jason rose slowly, making an obvious attempt to control his temper. "Since your husband has seen fit to abandon us for the good-bys, perhaps you should accompany me to the boat, Emily. I might need a hand on the slope, and there's the casting off as well."

Wishing to be finally done with it all, Emily quickly assented, and soon they were half-walking, half-sliding down the treacherous terrain to the tiny inlet. Smoot and Red had already managed to clamber aboard, but Pert was solicitously waiting on the ice-glazed rocks for his captain.

"Let me give you a hand, Cap'n."

Jason suddenly shoved Emily in front of himself. "It's not myself that needs a hand, but this lady, Pert."

Pert stared unbelievingly for a moment, unsure of what was happening. "But . . . "

"Blast! Smoot! Red! Give us a hand!"

Emily stood teetering on the jagged edge of the rocks, frozen seaweed splashing up around her ankles with the sea spray. What was happening?

"Jason! Have you lost your reason?" But almost before it was out of her mouth, strong arms were lifting her from above and behind, depositing her into the already heaving boat. In another second Jason and Pert had joined her and they were already too many yards out from the rocks of her island, about to plunge through the dangerous spume-filled currents. Emily was filled with horror, remembering the experience of her wedding night, and also, almost peripherally, remembering that she'd never learned how to swim. It was not one of the niceties expected of young ladies. "Jason!" she cried. "Get this boat back now! This instant!"

"Too late, my dear." And with a rush the boat pushed through the currents and was in the open sea.

"Dear God, help me! What are you trying to do with me?"

"Show you the world, of course. But first we shall start with the cave in which you expressed such an interest." He turned to Pert. "Take us there!" he barked out the order.

"But, Cap'n . . ."

"To the cave, Emmett! The rocks and the weather shall not stop us!" A strange gleam had entered his eye. His voice had a curious, trancelike quality to it. "We'll make it and back to the *Juliana* before daybreak. This falling snow is but a godsend for our purposes."

Emily stopped struggling and looked at Jason's men. They were staring uncomfortably at each other, then up at the cloudless, blue sky. Jason had gone off the deep end and was reliving the night of his shipwreck!

Pert gave Emily an apologetic look, shrugged his

shoulders, and motioned for Smoot, who was at the rudder, to change course for the far end of the island. Then he picked up a set of oars and stolidly began to row in unison with Red. Jason just sat and stared, unseeing, all the while keeping a tight grip on Emily's arm beside him. Suddenly, Jason began to laugh. It was a hollow, eerie laugh, and Emily could feel the shudder of shock it caused all through the boat's crew.

"A protective tariff, they call it! 'Tis a joke, eh, Emmett? Surely it will be our old-age protection. Congress itself has enacted it, and it makes for almost a better business than the slaves before the war. Certainly less smelly! No mouths to feed, either!" And he laughed again. "But 'tis deathly cold, Emmett. Have you one of those bottles loose to hand me for warmth?" He looked straight through Pert. "Come now, man! Surely you can forgo that oar for a moment!"

Pert calmly disengaged his oars and reached inside his jacket and beneath his sweater, emerging with a small flask which he carefully stretched to his captain. Jason pulled off the cap with his teeth, spit it out, and took a swig.

"'Tis decent port. Reminds me of the night we spent off Nazare. Those dark Portugee girls that came up off the sardine boats were something, eh? Dressed as if for a wake in their black shawls and gowns. But it weren't any funeral we had that night!" He laughed again, then took another drink before tossing the entire flask into the sea with a motion of disgust. "Some Scots' whiskey would warm me better this night, I think. And this cursed snow keeps falling. It's

170

impossible to see the shore. . . ." Suddenly he cried, "The rocks! The rocks, Emmett!"

Involuntarily, everyone in the boat, including Emily, jumped and stared in the direction he was pointing. They were really quite a safe distance off the island's shore, although now rounding its northern tip. But Jason was seeing a different vision.

"The opening to the cave! There it is! But the rocks! Watch the rocks, Emmett!" Suddenly he let out an unearthly scream, and collapsed.

Keith had not gone back to bed. He'd walked up to the bedroom, sat on the edge of the bed, then thinking better of it, pulled on the boots still in his hand and gotten up. He wandered restlessly around the confines of the room for a moment, touching the small personal things Emily had left out—the cloth she'd been sewing, the hairbrush on the dresser, a small, fancy bottle. He lifted it to his nose and sniffed, then quickly redeposited it with a reluctant grin. Unmistakably, the abominable scent of the night before! Still restive, he paced through the door, and across the hall where the nursery door was slightly ajar. He pushed it further open; gazed at the unfastened trunk, the confusion of clothing littering the floor, and recognized it as belonging to Patience. Why had Emily been immersing herself thus in his own sordid past? Had he forced her to this? Almost absent-mindedly, Keith began to pick up the litter and toss it into the trunk. There was a soft thunk. He looked down, then picked up the book that had been hidden in the folds of cloth. As if it had a will of its own, the book opened in his fingers, and he was glancing down at Patience's words, written in the unmistakable style of her own hand.

December 5, 1863—I feared the worst, and now it is certain. I am pregnant with his child. My days have been hell with the thought and pain of it. . . .

Incredulous, Keith could not tear his eyes away—not until unbelieving teardrops began to smudge the ink. "But it is done. He shall never know." Keith slammed the book shut and heaved it across the room with all his strength. This, then, was the effect he had upon women! Despairingly, he walked to the window. The tears still streamed down his face, making it almost impossible to clearly see the small procession making its way down to the sea. He wiped his eyes with his sleeve and felt the old, merciless throb return to his head. Then he looked out again. Two of the men were already in the boat, with the other sailor waiting on the rocks for the captain. Emily brought up the rear, her arm solicitously extended to help the injured man over the slickest spots.

Emily. How could he ever face her again, knowing she had read Patience's journal? Knowing she knew the total ignominy of his life? He moved to cover his face in his hands, then stopped, arrested by a curious sight. Emily teetering on the rocks. Emily being hoisted onto the longboat. Emily struggling, then subdued, as the boat shot through the inlet into the calmer waters of the sea.

For precious moments Keith stared before the information fully registered on his overwrought brain. Was it possible? From the movements of her body, even at that distance, it appeared she had not entered the boat willingly. Had the captain just abducted his wife within his own sight? Keith rubbed his eyes again, then looked. The boat was out of sight. *Gone.*

Old habits of self-recrimination and despair kept him rooted to the spot for another long moment. Then his whole body and soul revolted. No! He would not willingly let her go thus. She had read the journal and had still come to him last night—come to him, like a child in woman's dress, wanting desperately to please him. Yes, to please him, Keith Judson! No other woman had ever wanted that. He would not let her go! He spun around and raced down the stairs, stopping only for his greatcoat. *Please, God! Give me one final chance! Please!* The words repeated themselves over and over in his brain like a chant as he slid with death-defying speed over the icy path to the boathouse.

Keith wasted precious seconds trying to disengage the ice-encrusted ropes which held his dory safely intact in its wooden shelter. Then, rather than lose more time, he jumped in the boat and rode it down its slip, a wild, dangerous roller-coaster ride that ended with a huge, showering splash in the inlet. Cutting loose the final hindering ropes, he grasped the oars and pulled with all of his strength to the north, where he'd seen the *Juliana's* longboat disappear with his Emily.

Keith's dory barreled through the chaos of waves at the entry to the inlet, drenching him with water. He lost another moment rubbing the sea salt from his eyes with his sleeve, then spotted the longboat ahead. Like a man possessed, he pulled at the oars, quickly gaining on the other boat. He clearly saw its inhabitants now, Jason's men, the captain himself, and his Emily. They were all turned away, their attention fastened on something they spied on the rocky shore of the island. Silently, Keith closed the distance between the two boats. When only a few feet away, he lifted a single oar and struck a blow at Jason.

Jason screamed and slumped into Emily's arms. Suddenly everyone's attention was riveted again on him. Sweat was once more pouring down his face, turning now into flecks of ice. Emily held him a moment, unsure what to do next. Then she realized that the longboat's rhythm had changed. It was no longer moving forward, but was rocking gently with the waves. She looked up to find three pairs of eyes upon her. And a fourth, that of her own husband, from his dory nearby. She raised her eyes to his and her heart skipped several beats. Keith had come after her! This time he had really come after her! Praise the Lord! Joyfully, she smiled at him, pride and love lighting her face. His own eyes locked with hers, and she could see the heat and anger slowly dissipate. Keith broke the gaze with Emily and turned his head toward Jason's men.

"Turn back to the island, Pert!"

Pert paused a moment, then replied, "Aye, aye, sir." He gave another directive to Smoot and soon the boat was aboutface in the water, silently being pulled back.

"Pert?"

"Yes, ma'am?"

"I do not know of what mind your captain will be when he wakes. But when you get him back to the mainland, I suggest you pull up anchor on the *Juliana* as soon as possible and make for southern waters. Perhaps the islands around Cuba or Haiti . . . He seemed fond of them. The warmth will be the best healer for him now, I think."

"Yes, ma'am. But about the cave. . . ."

174

"I suspect somewhat about the cave, but as my husband says, it is no business of ours. Just take your captain, and make him well again. None of you are truly evil men, only opportunists. Keep him and yourselves in the south, out of these waters, and nothing further will be said about it. Do I make myself clear?"

"I understand, and I thankee for myself and the others. You are a fair woman, ma'am, a true Christian lady. 'Tis a pity you were not free to come with us. You'd make him a fine wife."

"Perhaps. But I belong with someone else."

Just then Jason began to move, to come to his senses. Slowly he sat up. He rubbed his face, his eyes, then gave a bewildered look about him.

"Pert! Smoot! Red! Wherever are we? And you"— he turned to Emily—"Miss Perkins, what in heaven's name are you doing out here?" Jason's men grinned at each other, then put on a burst of speed, while Jason himself continued to look bewildered. Thus the small retinue made its way back to the landing cove at Hazard Island.

The longboat had to stand offshore while Keith disembarked and raised his dory back up onto its slip. Only then did Pert pull in close to the rocks, just long enough for Keith's strong arms to bring Emily safely onto the solid craggy boulders of her island, and her husband's embrace. And there she remained engulfed, till at last Keith allowed her to turn and wave good-by to the fast-disappearing longboat.

Emily turned again to look into her husband's face. "Why, Keith! Are those tears?"

"Yes, woman, those are tears! Never frighten me again this way, do you hear? I thought I had lost you.

175

You. The only good thing that has ever come into my life.''

"Oh, Keith! You do care!"

"Care? I love you, woman! And I intend to prove it for the rest of our lives. But for now, I am taking you to bed. And it won't be sleep I'll be having on my mind!"

Arm in arm, they climbed the slope.

Then they were home. In their house, their bedroom, their bed. In each other's arms. Their first loving had had a certain exploratory tentativeness. This had none. Keith was neither anxious nor hurried.

Sitting with her on the side of the bed, he let down her hair, and surprisingly asked for her brush. Then he brushed her long tresses and it became a caress as he lingered over the glowing strands. Putting aside the brush, he blew away the fronds of his labor, his breath warming her.

"Thank God you came for me," she murmured.

"Today?" He nuzzled his cheek against hers.

"Today, yes. But most especially that other day, in my mother's kitchen.'' She fondled the thick hair at the back of his neck, then began tracing the outline of his shoulder blades with her finger.

"You knew, then?"

"I felt something, seeing you standing there, dripping, with that forlorn expression upon your face."

"Was I so pitiful, then?"

"Not pitiful. Commanding, yet beseeching. You had the courage to come and get me in that manner. It must not have been easy."

"One of the most difficult tasks of my life. If you had refused me. . . ." His voice was strangely hoarse.

"But I did not," she sighed.

"No. You did not, and I thank God for that. But that will be quite enough talk for now. I do believe it is time to assert myself again!"

He reached to draw her much closer, sheltering her close to his heart and beneath the eiderdown quilt. And there they remained for the duration of the long winter's afternoon, and many more to come.

CHAPTER 10

Nov. 24. First big gale of the season arrived from NNE last night. Ice caked heavily on lantern windows. Keeper's wife in labor all night.

Keith had every pot in the house filled with boiling water. Undoubtedly it was more than needed, but he would take no chances with his wife and his baby. He'd tried to take Emily off the island, said it might be best for her to have the child with her mother and sisters and the doctor at hand in East Egg. She'd have none of it. He remembered the conversation with a smile.

"Really, Keith. You expect me to go ashore now, just as the weather is about to worsen?"

"But if there are complications?"

"There will be no complications. I am young and strong. We have the birthing book the doctor gave us. We have both studied it well. The worst complication would be having me stuck in East Egg, and the bay frozen over, and not being able to see you till the spring. I could not stand that."

"It would be harder for me. Not knowing about you and the child . . ."

"So. It is decided, then. I stay."

He had patted her huge stomach lovingly and kissed her on the cheek. "You will stay. And God will help us."

It had been the most wonderful spring and summer of Keith's life. In late April small wildflowers and herbs had burst out all over the island. His seedling trees had survived, and he'd had a boatload of soil hauled in to start a garden. Emily's father had returned from his long voyage and spent several glorious weeks with them, Emily delighted with the instant rapport that sprang up between the two men.

The weather had been mild, the sea calm, and they'd constructed traps and gone lobstering, then sat late into the night picking at the shells while Daniel Perkins related his adventures. Her father had brought them the gift of a chessboard and figures, and during other nights he had instructed them in the mysteries of the game, commenting that many were the times on his long journeys when chess had kept him sane through weeks of doldrums with no wind to move the ship, no whales, and no way of knowing how his family fared at home. He thought perhaps there might be such periods on their island as well, and Keith had nodded his silent assent.

It had been while her father was still with them that Emily had made the momentous announcement of her pregnancy, first privately to Keith, then to her father over dinner together. To say that both men were delighted was an understatement. Emily's father had decided then and there that his forthcoming voyage would be of shorter duration.

"You know, Emily, I've enjoyed my voyages, but I have missed too much of the growing up of you and the other girls. I think I should very much like to be a bigger part of my grandchild's life."

Emily had given her father a loving hug.

"This next trip will not last for years, then?"

"No. And it is not only you who is to be the deciding factor, either." He paused to look at Keith. "I daresay you've heard tell of this new oil that they are bringing out of the ground now?"

"Yes. The visit from the Lighthouse Service tender last month had the lampist talking of it to no end. It seems most of the lights will be switched over in the next few years. He said it was cheaper and more readily available."

Captain Perkins had sighed. "Too true. It is the same story everywhere. And the whales are not as easy to find as in the old days. I fear we may have fished them out. Poor beasts. There is something quite noble about them. Last summer we followed the diminishing herds north to Greenland and the taking was so poor that I regret we had to slaughter some of the Eskimos' personal quarry—the narwhal." He stopped for a moment, bemused in the memory. "Have you ever heard of this creature?" At their negative nods he continued. "It is small for the whale family, and almost mythical in appearance. You know about the unicorn, that gentle, horned horse somewhat storied by the old Europeans?"

"I do not, Father," said Emily, "but it sounds most wonderful."

"It is, indeed. They say that it will allow itself to be seen and communicated with only by the most purehearted and innocent of maidens." He paused again, ruminating. "I think, perhaps, Emily dear, that if there really were unicorns in this world, they might choose to talk with you."

Emily blushed becomingly. "In my current delicate condition, Father?"

He smiled and stopped toying with his spoon. "Pureheartedness is a state of mind, after all, daughter, a kind of loving glow from within. I think you shall always pass that test." He took her hand for a moment, then cleared his throat in minor embarrassment. Keith just puffed on his pipe and beamed. "But I travel far from the point of my story. I fear you shall believe me aging badly, perhaps beginning to dodder. . . ."

Emily laughed. "You, Father? Never!"

He ran a hand through his thick, graying hair. "I'll be fifty-two next month, after all. Married and started the family a bit late . . ." He glanced up and saw the look of amusement on Keith's face. "But I did beat you, my boy!"

Keith grinned. "About that narwhal, sir. . . ."

"Well said! We were up in the northern waters, poking about to no avail for the killer whales that feed off them, getting closer and closer to the incredible cliffs of ice that exist even in Greenland's summer, spotting an occasional kayak or two . . . when up shot an unbelievable apparition. The beast was undoubtedly a whale, but it had a *horn* on it, perhaps fifteen feet long or more, protruding from its snout. The most incredible thing. . . . But I repeat myself. I did not wish to pursue such a creature, but the men were wild

181

for the hunt. . . ." He paused again, a far-off look in his eye. "It was the most beautiful ivory, with dark bands spiraling around the cream. The world is filled with such wonders. . . . One of the natives to whom we later spoke managed to convey to us that the narwhal's ivory horn was considered sacred, and used in their religious rituals." He stopped again.

"Then what happened, Father?"

"Well, we'd caught this beauty, and several others, and were beginning the butchering when we found ourselves surrounded by kayaks, each Eskimo with a harpoon in hand—aimed at us." He swallowed some coffee, returned the thick cup to the table.

Emily was leaning forward, the image of the whaler floating in a barren sea of ice, surrounded by fur-clad, hostile natives strong in her mind. "And then? . . ."

Daniel Perkins laughed richly at the look in her eyes. "And then we compromised. We presented them with the horns and half of the skin and blubber. They returned to land chanting and planning a feast. We hoisted sail and set out for southern waters. As the Good Book tells us, there is a time for all things, and I felt in my heart that the time was ripe to be leaving the land of the Eskimos."

"A wonderfully understated tale, Captain." A gleam of humor was in Keith's eyes. "I would have given much in my youthful days to have seen as much."

"And now?" asked Emily's father.

"I no longer have need of the wanderlust or the dreams. My heart's desire is here." And he cast a loving glance at Emily.

Daniel Perkins scraped his chair out from under himself and rose. "Care to join me for a walk around your domain before retiring, Emily? I know Keith must tend to his light. And a fine thing, too, for many's the night that I have blessed all lighthouse keepers from my opposite position on the sea." He glanced out the kitchen window. "Although there will be no distress on this fine evening. Not even much wind blowing by the looks of it."

Keith followed his gaze. "No, sir. Just a few wicks to be trimmed. But perhaps you'd favor me with your company awhile after Emily has retired?"

"Indeed. A fine night for yarning, while the ship sails through soft and gentle seas."

"And what about me, then?" asked Emily, not willing to miss a moment of the camaraderie.

"You, my dear, will be taking your needed rest. Never forget that you must sleep as well as eat for two now!" And Keith kissed her cheek softly and strode out to his airie.

She watched him go and quickly finished the tidying up of the kitchen. "Well, then, Father, we'd best be about our walk, for you've heard my orders read to me."

On another evening as Emily, bursting with energy, was allowed to join the men for "yarning" in the tower. Her father had been wondering aloud over the recent War Between the States and Keith had broken his silence on the subject for the first time.

"Being a soldier, sir, is not unlike hunting the whales, I'll be thinking. Both require the killer instinct, although to make the leap from beast to man is hard, indeed. Hard and treacherous. For once some men have had the taste of another's blood. . . ." His limbs stiffened with remembrance and he began to

pace the confined space, the tensions not seen in past
months unconsciously returning.

Emily herself stiffened, and made a small motion to
rise and comfort, but her father stopped her with his
hand, his eyes upon Keith.

"The cause was a just one, it is true, but one
sometimes wonders if any cause be worth such
pain. . . ." And then it came out, in a smooth flow of
words. "After a battle, finding myself whole, I must
need walk. I would begin, of course, like others,
poking my head above the position, musket smoke in
my nostrils, peering out over a field of carnage with a
fog of cannon and shot fumes floating in a haze above
all, just beginning to lift with the fresh breezes, and
the sun filtering through in spots, outlining a broken
wagon here, an overturned cannon there, bodies
strewn helter-skelter, arms and legs akimbo. And a
soft keening rising above it all, as if the angels were
crying at the folly of men . . . Such a walk I took one
day, stumbling blindly over the carcasses of horse and
man alike, seeing neither in my inner turmoil till I
came to the edge of the battlefield and found a
somewhat stout, bearded, middle-aged man preparing
a camera to picture the chaos.

" 'What in God's name are you doing?' I shouted at
him. 'Do you not hear the cries of the wounded and
dying? And you of able body to help?'

" 'But I am helping, Lieutenant,' he calmly answered. 'I am helping the dying bodies and the dying
souls, too, like yours. I am making a record of the
carnage. Such a record as the world has never seen.
When they look upon my pictures, do you think they
will be able to stomach the like ever again?'

"And he calmly propped me against a tree and got

184

on with his business. Later I found that his name was Brady, Matthew Brady. The soldiers got used to seeing his photographic buggy everywhere. They called it the 'What-is-it?' wagon and they would joke about 'that grand picture-maker' who took chances equal to theirs. We met face to face again at the second battle of Bull Run. He had lost his wagon and himself and was as scared as the rest of us, wandering around the battlefield in his long linen duster, unarmed. I offered him my sword and, as he took it, he looked me in the eye carefully. 'So, the body has not yet died, Lieutenant.' "Then he was gone." Keith let out a sigh, and limply leaned against a window to stare out at the stars.

"Matthew Brady . . . the folio edition of pictures from Jason," whispered Emily.

"Yes. I have leafed through it in the study," commented her father. "It is a most powerful testament." He looked at her. "To bed, daughter. Your husband will be wanting a bit of privacy now, I judge."

The three of them were out in the dory, checking lobster pots. Away from the tricky currents of the island the sea was like glass. Emily had her hand over the side, dipping it in the cool water, occasionally playfully splashing a bit at the working men, sweating in the effort of pulling the deep lines. Her father frowned at an empty trap, then sent it scuttling back to the bottom.

"I do believe this is harder work than whaling." He wiped his forehead with his neckerchief.

"I am sure that it is, Father, for when has the

captain gone after the whale, or flayed it?" teased Emily.

"Do not be so quick to say that lightly, my girl," cautioned Keith.

"Indeed," added her father. "Always remember that there are two kinds of people in this world, those who receive orders and those who give them. At times I have been very sure that to give orders is the more difficult of the two." He made a motion to pick up the oars, but Keith waved him aside and rowed strongly toward their next floating marker.

Emily's father began to reminisce. "I had a mutiny on my hands once, about the time you were being born . . . I never did manage to be at hand for any of your births, only the beginnings. . . ." he chuckled. "It was really only a half-baked mutiny, looking back, but it seemed trouble enough then. We'd been at sea several months and were off the coast of South America, near as spit to Brazil by the charts. We'd had only one kill on the voyage thus far, and in the equatorial heat and doldrums the men's tempers flared. They'd have none of my preaching, nor temporizing, either—and I did a bit of both in my younger days before I learned that actions speak louder than words. My first mate was a Cape Verdian I'd never sailed with. Neither had I hired him, since neither the hiring nor the boat were then mine. He gathered his Portugee mates about him and made a try for the ship. I caught on and scotched it in time, but then I had half a crew filled with hatred and distrust."

"What did you do, Father?"

"The only thing I could think of. I sailed for the shore and deposited them in Brazil amongst a common language. Of course there was a fair piece of jungle they had to navigate before they'd actually find anyone else to communicate with!" He smiled, then turned serious. "I've had those souls on my conscience for twenty years, not knowing if they made it or not. But there was no other choice. That was my least successful voyage. Had to turn around and sail back home for a fresh crew." He paused. "Which is why your eldest sister was born not much more than a year after you. The rest were at neater intervals. Gave your mother a chance to catch up on her scrubbing." He smiled wryly and put his back into hauling up another lobster pot.

"Father?"

"Yes?"

"If Mother had been a little . . . different . . . would you have been always away on such long voyages?"

"A whaling man has got to follow the whales. But . . . ouch! This little red devil—excuse me, daughter—this, this lobster took a fair piece of my finger." He glared at the beast ruefully. "Enjoy it, for we'll be enjoying you tonight!" He glanced back at Emily. "Perhaps. Maybe not. I cannot say."

Keith steadied the boat and watched the two of them, saying nothing.

"Father?"

He was nursing his wound now, wrapping his neckerchief around it to stop the trickle of blood. "Yes, daughter?"

"You are still a young man. What will you do now that the whales are no longer running well, and the killing of them is no longer of much purpose if this new oil is to take their place?"

He finished his ministrations and threw the pot, freshly baited, back into the sea. "Luckily, I am my

187

own master. The ship I own, too. I have been seriously thinking of taking it to Bath for refitting on my next return, to suit, perhaps, the coastal trade. My trips would not be as long, and I could be home maybe three for four times a year.''

Emily looked at if she might clap her hands, or even tip the dory in an attempt to embrace her father. She did neither, but the pleasure shown on her face. Keith bent into the oars, heading for home. And after Captain Daniel Perkins departed the following day, Emily was not as depressed by the leavetaking as Keith had feared.

The spring had turned into a delightfully crisp and clear island summer. They'd had other visitors to enliven this golden time as well. A crew had come in June to rebuild the bell tower. They had camped down in Keith's tool shop for a month while they built from scratch, this time out of sturdy, storm-defying island stones, and made other major repairs to the place.

One of these changes had been at Keith's suggestion and expense—the installation of a genuine, imported, water-chamber into one corner of the pantry. And while they were laying in pipes for that anyway, he had them turn the kitchen's dry sink into a wet one. Emily had been delighted with the new conveniences, and had not minded the extra cooking for the six workers at all, even in her current condition.

And the evenings had been pleasant, the men accepting himself and Emily in an easy camaraderie.

And July! July had been a month for the stars. Night after night he and Emily had spent gazing, exploring the heavens. Then sleeping past noon in each other's arms once the light had been extinguished. . . .

August and September had been filled with their own wonder as he daily watched his wife blossom before his eyes .

And when the winds of October came and Emily could sleep only fitfully by night, she would come up to his tower and they would read Dickens or Melville or Scott together.

Keith beamed as he brought himself back to earth and manhandled a pot of steaming water up the stairs. He had certainly gotten himself a fine wife. No question. He paused at the top of the landing to peek into the waiting nursery. All autumn, when the rains had come, Emily had spent her days in there, lovingly painting bright animals and friendly sea creatures romping together across the walls.

There was her father's narwhal, a grin on its face as it cavorted with a mischievous unicorn, and a lovely mermaid, whose countenance and tresses were the image of Emily's, watched lovingly from her perch atop a rock on the sidelines. And that lion on the beach beamed through its whiskers with the face of Daniel Perkins. But what's this? He edged closer to the large tiger emerging from the forest onto the beach. He'd not noticed before, but its visage was his own, and its stripes—its stripes were words! Keith bent to the stripes and began to read:

Tyger! Tyger! burning bright
In the forests of the night:
What immortal hand or eye,
Dare frame thy fearful symmetry?

189

He stared in wonder till the steam from the pot scorched his fingers and he retreated to the edge of the round rug by the door, the rug Emily had made to keep the floor warm for when their baby began to crawl and explore. A last look at the ceiling where a sun and a moon smiled down on the crib and cradle he had built. They were both warmly lined with quilts and blankets from Mother Perkins. He stopped beaming when he remembered his current errand and hurried into their bedroom, setting the hot pot upon the floor.

Emily was dripping with sweat, but she smiled up at him, uncomplainingly. There had been no screams the entire night. It was at first difficult for him to understand, instinctively comprehending as he did the exertion she was undergoing. But his Emily, bless her, had a newfangled theory about all that. They'd talked it over at length. It was a well-known fact that women bring children into the world in pain and suffering. His Emily had said nonsense to all that. Her baby had been conceived in joy, and she would see to it that it came into the world joyfully as well. Then there had been the long talks with her father, with him describing birthing ceremonies he'd witnessed in certain South Seas islands. The natives had gathered around the expectant mother, chanting in rising rhythms with her contractions, partaking in the event, helping the mother to "breathe" the baby out. He and Emily had not known the chants, but had devised their own breathing rhythms.

Keith stood now by Emily's side, and she grasped his hand.

"How goes it, my love?" He bent and with his free

hand wiped her brow with a damp cloth. Then he offered her a sip of blackberry tea.

She smiled again, a bit weakly with the effort. "Soon. Our child is almost here."

Together they worked, as they did all things together. And in a few minutes, they were rewarded with first a tiny wet head, and then a squirming body. Keith lifted the child into his huge hands and a smile broke out.

"A boy, Emily! God has given us a son!" Quickly he performed the tasks of drying and wrapping the child in the soft blankets Emily had so lovingly stitched. As their son's first cry rang out, loud and clear, Emily gave a gasp. Keith rushed to her side with the bundle.

"What is it?" the concern rising in his voice.

"It is not over, Keith! The contractions still come."

"Perhaps it is the afterbirth?"

"No. No. Quickly now. Lay the boy by my side."

Keith did as he was bade, then returned to the foot of the bed.

"Another head! Emily! It is twins!" And in a moment Keith was ministering to the second child. And his grin was even wider.

"A girl! It is a girl, Emily!"

Tears of joy glistened in her eyes. "Thank You, Lord," she whispered softly. Then she gathered her son to her breast. "Bring her quickly, Keith. My breasts are beginning to feel full. The nourishment is good for them, and they will get acquainted at once!"

Soon Keith was sitting by her side in a daze, admiring the tiny heads with their silken, strawberry-blond hair and tightly chenched fists. Such a doubly blessed event he could scarcely take in. Surely there was enough wood left in his shop for another cradle and crib. But he would have to build fast.

"What shall we name them, Keith?"

"The boy shall be named Daniel, after your father."

She smiled. "And the girl?"

"I've always fancied the name Suzanne."

She smiled. "Suzanne it is then."

His eyes grew misty as he watched his wife and babes.

"Ah, Emily, this house has been in need of more light than my feeble beam could supply." He paced restlessly as he attempted to frame the long thoughts born of solitary nights. "And it has come to me at last. The day you entered my life you brought with you a joy that I have only now begun to fathom. It is that inner light that carried you through the unfortunate events of our early days together, that has transformed this lonely outpost into a true haven, that has made this day"—and he choked on the words—"the happiest of my life. How I do love you, my Emily, and now I can love God, too, because I have seen Him in you."

And then he bent to kiss his family—love, joy and a new humility glowing in his eyes.

ABOUT THE AUTHOR

KATHLEEN KARR is a graduate of the Catholic University of America and Providence College with an M.A. in English Literature. More recently she has been professionally involved in the exhibition end of the motion picture business as General Manager and Advertising Director for the Circle Theaters in Washington, D.C. She occasionally teaches at local universities.

Mrs. Karr is the mother of two young children and lives in Washington in a turn-of-the-century townhouse that she and her husband have restored.

A Letter To Our Readers

Dear Reader:

Pioneering is an exhilarating experience, filled with opportunities for exploring new frontiers. The Zondervan Corporation is proud to be the first major publisher to launch a series of inspirational romances designed to inspire and uplift as well as to provide wholesome entertainment. In order that we might better contribute to your reading enjoyment, we would appreciate your taking a few minutes to respond to the following questions and return to:

> Anne Severance, Editor
> Serenade/Saga Books
> 749 Templeton Drive
> Nashville, Tennessee   37205

1. Did you enjoy reading LIGHT OF MY HEART?

    ☐ Very much. I would like to see more books by this author!
    ☐ Moderately
    ☐ I would have enjoyed it more if _____

2. Where did you purchase this book? _____

3. What influenced your decision to purchase this book?

    ☐ Cover   ☐ Back cover copy
    ☐ Title   ☐ Friends
    ☐ Publicity   ☐ Other _____

4. Please rate the following elements from 1 (poor) to 10 (superior).

☐ Heroine   ☐ Plot
☐ Hero   ☐ Inspirational theme
☐ Setting   ☐ Secondary characters

5. Which settings would you like to see in future Serenade/Saga Books?

_____ _____

_____ _____

6. What are some inspirational themes you would like to see treated in future books?

_____ _____

_____ _____

7. Would you be interested in reading other Serenade/Serenata or Serenade/Saga Books?

☐ Very interested
☐ Moderately interested
☐ Not interested

8. Please indicate your age range:

☐ Under 18   ☐ 25–34   ☐ 46–55
☐ 18–24   ☐ 35–45   ☐ Over 55

9. Would you be interested in a Serenade book club? If so, please give us your name and address:

Name _____

Occupation _____

Address _____

City _____ State _____ Zip _____

Serenade Saga Books are inspirational romances in historical settings, designed to bring you a joyful, heart-lifting reading experience.

Serenade Saga books available in your local book store:

#1 SUMMER SNOW, Sandy Dengler
#2 CALL HER BLESSED, Jeanette Gilge
#3 INA, Karen Baker Kletzing
#4 JULIANA OF CLOVER HILL,
     Brenda Knight Graham
#5 SONG OF THE NEREIDS, Sandy Dengler
#6 ANNA'S ROCKING CHAIR,
     Elaine Watson
#7 IN LOVE'S OWN TIME,
     Susan C. Feldhake
#8 YANKEE BRIDE, Jane Peart

Watch for other books in both the *Serenade Saga* and *Serenade Serenata* (contemporary) series coming soon:
#10 (September) SMOKY MOUNTAIN SUN-RISE, Yvonne Lehman (Serenata)
#10 (October) LOVE BEYOND SURRENDER, Susan C. Feldhake (Saga)
#11 (November) GREENGOLD AUTUMN, Donna Fletcher Crow (Serenata)
#11 (December) ALL THE DAYS AFTER SUN-DAY, Jeanette Gilge (Saga)